The DRAGONS of EDEN

IRONY SADE

The Dragons of Eden
©2024 Irony Sade

print ISBN: 979-8-35094-028-2
ebook ISBN: 979-8-35094-029-9

PART ONE:

The Navigator

Eons had passed. An eternity of darkness. She was cold, achingly cold, almost to the point of senescence, but for the first time in ages she felt the tickle of light from distant stars.

The Navigator roused her lesser functions. She absorbed the dust coating her forward eyes and integrated their knowledge. Stars swirled before her, distant still, but distinct. No longer a smudged ancestral memory slipping behind clouds of gas, but a brilliant swirl of life. An alien galaxy.

She had done it. Something none of her kind had believed possible. She allowed herself a moment of smug accomplishment, then cleaned the dust from her rearward eyes.

Home was gone. Her own galaxy was no longer visible, even to her. Unknowable distance and the gas between stars obscured it.

She had calculated a trajectory many orders of magnitude beyond the longest journey of her memory, and she had survived. Her ancient namesake would be proud.

The Navigator looked inward, checking her reserves. Her scales were iced over, frozen from the depths of space. Her body was stuporous, starved, every heat sink drained to protect her vital heart. Even her stolen uranium was dissipating, pockets of radium and lead slowly replacing the blistering weapon she had wrested from the Destroyer at the end of their terrible struggle. The Navigator allowed herself another moment of self-satisfaction. The Destroyer was imprisoned, trapped inside her own heart, with not even starlight to sustain her. She, the Navigator, would survive.

She opened new eyes, instructed them to record and calculate every star, every swirl of dust, every well of gravity in the flat spiral galaxy unfolding before her. She ran her impossible calculation again and checked it against the data she had absorbed. Her trajectory was sound. It would take time to absorb enough light to adjust her course, but time was not a problem. The Navigator smiled in her heart and slept on.

DANNY

The crystals hit his bloodstream and everything was good. No pain. No fear. No second thoughts. It was like he had been hunched over his whole life and could suddenly stand straight. He exhaled, slowly leaning back into the enveloping couch. He was alone and everything was perfect.

Ten minutes, he thought. *Just ten minutes, then I'll go back. Then I can be Danny Orion for another night. Then I can blast out the music fast and loose. Check out the girls and ham it up for all those morons who paid good money to see us live. Just give me ten minutes first.*

He lay still, marveling at the perfection of his own heartbeat, the distracting flow of his own breath. He watched the muted lights glow and shimmer around the private shuttle docked to the space station where the rest of the Supernovas were working the crowd. Some pipsqueak local band was opening for them. The Asteroid something. Some power move of his father's, no doubt. Nothing to do with talent.

Thump.

The high was starting to fade. Too soon. Always too soon. He felt the loose, fluid lethargy permeating his limbs. The zone. Fast hands, slow eyes. Get the brain out of the way and let the magic flow. It was never as good as the first time, but it would do.

Thump, thump.

Shit. Were they starting without him? Impossible. They wouldn't have the balls. He *was* the band. Everyone knew that.

Danny staggered upright, untangling his coat. The embroidered leather dragged at his bare chest, sparkling filaments of sensation from the crystalline high, distracting him again.

There were more bass thumps and singing. Terribly off key.

He swaggered to the airlock and threw it open. Screams. Not singing. Hair-raising, bowel-watering screams. Acrid smoke with the nauseating scent of burnt flesh pushed him back.

Figures streamed past him, bloodied, blackened. Expensive rags and smeared makeup, frantic eyes, and flailing limbs. Some dozens piled through the airlock, into the shuttle, trampling others in their desperation.

"It's collapsing!" he heard among the chaos. "Bombs! They had bombs!"

Danny stared beyond the airlock down a long corridor of glass and mirrors. The smoke was being sucked away. Glass was shattering in the distance, vanishing backward into the void. People raced toward him, reaching, desperate for the open door.

"Help us!" A blond woman screamed, staggering forward, only steps away.

He slammed the airlock. He was too high to pilot, but he threw himself into the forward cabin and fumbled through the disengagement sequence, separating the shuttle from the collapsing station. His hands danced through the patterns, his eyes lagging behind.

"Oh, my god! It's Danny!" someone gasped.

"We're saved! Danny saved us!"

He stared through the windows. The shuttle drifted, free from the fragments of collapsing glass and metal. There was no more station. Chaos confronted him. Bodies drifted through empty space, decked out and painted. Some of their flickering ornamental beads were still glowing in the darkness. He could see nothing but the blond woman's face, her desperate eyes, her hands reaching for safety. Danny Orion tipped forward and vomited across the screens.

IVAN

"You will make us proud."

Ivan glanced down at the Rudnikov. He had feared the man through his childhood, hated him through adolescence. For the past ten years he had regarded him as a cunning enemy, one he had to outthink, out work, outmaneuver, in order to survive. Now, in the final moments, Ivan found he pitied him.

"You are the best of us," the Rudnikov continued, not meeting his eye. "Strong. Smart. Brave. You are educated and accomplished."

Their footsteps echoed along the cold metal walls. The soft, slow boom of Ivan's heels. The thump-click-drag of the supervisor's ruined leg and ever-present cane.

The Rudnikov coughed once. He always coughed once. An unpleasant rattle with a quick laryngeal bob. Ivan strongly suspected the man had an incurable tumor. He also expected he would be found dead, frozen stiff at his desk, still glowering into the dim tunnels before he ever stepped down to acknowledge a replacement.

"I know what they say about Novgorod among the stars. We are brutal. Uneducated. Simple miners."

The chill bit at Ivan, even after decades underground. Frozen vapors clung to the walls, thin stalactites of blue where copper gave way to the corrosive fumes. Pink streaks of cobalt, pale green patches of barium chloride, all frozen to the rusting walls. Lifelong friends he hoped never to miss. His right arm had goosebumps under his heavy coat. His left was immune.

"But you! You will prove them wrong. You will board this ship and prove to Exodus, to the whole interstellar community, that we are more than that."

They stopped at the final airlock. Beyond was the elevator that would take him to the surface, to the shuttle, to the waiting ship. So many years of work and study just to pass this door.

"We will be dead and gone, still trapped in the ice, long before you awake," the Rudnikov stated. "But you! You will make us proud."

They shook hands, the supervisor gripping until his arm trembled, Ivan matching his grip with careful strength.

Then the door shut. Air hissed. The lift began to rise. Ivan felt himself begin to smile. He was free.

BADGER

They were not supposed to dream. Stasis was nothing. A blink of the eye. A peaceful nap, be it ten years or two hundred.

Bullshit. Maybe it was like that for other people. Civilized people. Ones who had the luxury of shutting off their brains.

Badger dreamt. He was crouched in darkness, teeth gleaming. A curved knife in his right hand, a charged disrupter in his left. Something hunted him in the night. Or maybe he was hunting it.

There was a wordless howl. The percussive thump of artillery. He sprinted forward on silent feet, seeking blood or shelter. He would be sane when he awoke, or act that way. For now, he hunted.

THE *ABEONA*

The *Abeona* was worried. Seven hundred and forty-two functions were running smoothly. Three were not. She watched the data stream trail off again from her latest planetary probe. Sensible data became glitchy, became gibberish, became silence. It was as if she were listening to the signals of a probe at the failing end of its life as rust, moisture, and environmental trauma destroyed its data-collecting array, ruined its transmitter, and ate into its battery. She knew these sounds from probes dropped into hostile environments, uninhabitable worlds that she scouted for mineral wealth while passing by with her sleeping cargo.

Her probes were designed to last a month on a hostile world, to send back reliable data while slowly being destroyed by their environment. This was not a hostile world, and they had only lasted a week. She ran the data stream again, checking it against the others, mapping the speed of breakdown. She checked it against the test functions of her un-deployed probes in the hold. Then she checked the other 742 functions that were still running smoothly. Finally, she checked her own self-diagnostics to make sure she was not somehow corrupted.

The *Abeona* was not an emotional being. She was not programmed as such, nor could she afford to be, given her function. She knew her limits. The protocol was clear, however expensive. She made her decision.

Outside her hull, solar panels deployed smoothly, oriented toward the new yellow sun. The gaping maw of her antimatter engines sat silent. Below her a blue-green marble of a world shimmered benignly in the darkness.

DRUMMER

He was awake, but nothing else. No light, no fear, no sense of place. No feeling of pain or pressure, no taste of morning breath. Just gradual awareness.

"Mr. Drummer?"

Was that him? The name sounded familiar. So did the voice. He had heard it somewhere before.

"Mr. Drummer?"

"Yes?" he responded. "Maybe?" Slight panic then. His mouth did not move; his tongue did not slide. He was not sure he had a tongue. He could not feel a thing.

"Good morning, Mr. Drummer. I have awakened your mind in stasis. Your body is still asleep. Do not be alarmed."

He felt no rush of blood, no tingling of fingers, no copper tang of panic on his tongue. No hormones, then, or no body.

"Well, now I'm alarmed. Who are you?"

"I am the *Abeona*, the colony ship you took passage on. Congratulations! We have arrived at Eden."

Memory began creeping back. Eden: a fresh green world on the edge of the galaxy. Trees and rivers, oceans and volcanoes. A fresh start for young families seeking to escape their overburdened worlds and spread humanity to the stars. Or for someone running from their old life with no plans of going back. He had volunteered, he remembered. In fact, he had paid extra. He had called in quite a lot of favors, faking medical records, buying references, and donating all his assets to Exodus for this chance. His father had been furious.

"Oh. Good." His thoughts were beginning to move properly again. "Then why haven't you woken me all the way up?"

There was a pause. Now that he was more alert, there were pauses at both ends of the *Abeona's* speech, as if the ship was distracted or choosing her words carefully.

"There appears to be something wrong with the planet."

"Oh."

"It may not be serious. The atmosphere is breathable; the water is clean. My probes have not detected any serious toxins and several indigenous plants appear edible for humans and livestock.

Unfortunately, none of my probes have remained functional long enough to complete the mapping process. They have all broken down more rapidly than the atmospheric conditions would predict. I have not found any discrete dangers, but I am unable to verify Eden as safe."

"So you send more probes or you go to the backup world."

"I did send more probes. They also broke down. I do not have an infinite supply. The costs of changing course to Svarga Loka are significant. In this situation a human reconnaissance is recommended by protocol."

Drummer felt his heart sinking, metaphorically.

"I would like you to be part of the first human expedition to Eden, to see if it is safe for the remaining passengers," the *Abeona* continued. "If it is confirmed safe, you will be rewarded with a doubling of your resource allocation and have the honor of being among the first to the surface of a new world. If it is not safe, you will be evacuated to stasis and given a doubling of your resource allocation when we arrive at Svarga Loka."

"No. Why me? Why can't someone else go down and wake me when it is confirmed safe?"

The ship paused. "You have a high survival potential, Mr. Drummer. I estimate that you are one of the twenty passengers most likely to both identify any dangers on the surface and to survive them."

"High survival potential. You mean I got lucky once?"

"You were not lucky." The ship paused again. Drummer detected something almost sorrowful in her tone. "You survived tragedy through clear thinking and quick action, where many persons who were more accomplished and better trained did not. I do not need specialists for this endeavor. The engineers, botanists, biotechnologists, and farmers can come later. I need people who will see what is in front of them and survive."

"Expendable people without valuable skills. Like me." Drummer paused. This was not for him. He was no hero. He was the least reliable person he knew. "What if I say no?"

"Then you will go back into stasis with the knowledge that the reconnaissance team will be made up of people without your survival potential, and they will be the ones responsible for deciding if Eden is safe."

"You do know who I am, right?"

"I know your inclusion in this mission was irregular. I know you purchased your spot by lobbying Exodus. But that deal was with them. It bought you passage, nothing else. I have complete autonomy regarding my passengers and their safety. You are one of those I believe is best suited to this task."

Drummer thought, invisible fingers tapping out a complex rhythm, until he realized he had no fingers. He had wanted a change, hadn't he? A chance to prove he was someone else? And money was money, whatever form it took.

"Double my allocation? And I can still be Mr. Drummer?"

"Of course," said the ship. "Your original name is sealed at your request. Every record on this ship refers to Drummer."

"All right. I'll do it."

"Very good. Stand by for your awakening. Look for Fable, the communications leader. She will give you your assignment."

THE NAVIGATOR

More time had passed. Something was tugging at her. The Navigator roused herself again and felt the faint change in the pattern of space, gravity pulling her slightly off course.

With an effort she awakened more of herself, internalizing her forward eyes again and assimilating their data. She was on the fringes of the new galaxy at last, passing between burned-out giants and un-kindled clouds of interstellar gas. Her eyes had built the foundations of a map of this alien spiral, and she rapidly filled it in, combining their observations with her own nuanced calculations. She set the model to spinning in her heart and began the merciless, meticulous updates her line was famous for. When was the last time one of her kind had had a new galaxy to map?

She opened eyes all over her meridians, squeezing a frugal burst of energy from the decaying uranium. Her shell had absorbed enough light to be malleable, but her reserves were limited. Feeding off these dead giants would be a zero-sum game. They were first-generation stars with weak minerals. She would have to head inward.

The Navigator spun herself through the slowly expanding map, predicting courses and calculating costs. *Too slow. Too risky. There.*

A third-generation star glittered yellow in the middle distance. Still far by normal standards, but nothing like the gulfs she had already traversed. She opened a new eye, dedicating its crystals to spectrography, and waited. Data trickled in. She felt the gravity of the dead giants pulling her slowly in, shifting her calculations. She waited, biding her time.

Silicon. Sulfur. Gold. That would do. With a calculated effort she collected the clumps of lead and polonium into a sphere. She funneled small pockets of gas into a cavity. At the appropriate moment, she let the heavy mass eject, blasted out by the gaseous effluent.

Her course shifted. She slipped out of the gravity well of the dead giants, heading for the yellow sun. From here on she would have to be more involved.

IVAN

Ivan glanced up from his tablet, matching faces to names. The shuttle jounced and rocked slightly as it moved through the airlocks separating it from orbit. It smelled of clean oil and stale air. His companions smelled of sweat and fear.

He glanced at the tablet again.

Fable: Communication leader. He scanned her brief biography and glanced around the cabin. This one was easy. A stout woman with iron grey hair sat strapped in across the aisle. Her face was composed, but slightly green. She was not used to shuttles.

Beside her sat a younger man, slim built, good looking, with brown hair. He had a smooth face but old eyes. He did not seem to notice the motions of the shuttle, but his hands and one foot tapped separate unconscious rhythms against the bench. He had a distant, almost haunted look. His clothing looked expensive but deliberately generic. Ivan glanced back at the names. Nothing specific to go on. One biography was as generic as the man. *Drummer.* He put a mental question mark beside the name and moved on.

So far he had matched five of his companions to their brief biographies. The rest were out of sight or difficult to pin down. He committed the profiles to memory. Many seemed deliberately vague. Two read simply "Scout." His own biography was comically brief, considering the work and sacrifice he had put in to earn this opportunity. There were no surnames, no stories. No hint of history or struggle, the reasons each of them had for being here, or the real reasons behind those. He did note one commonality—none of these people had family on the ship.

We are expendable, he thought grimly. He had deduced as much from the *Abeona* when she had offered him this spot. It was irritating to have come so far and be back where he had started, but it was familiar territory.

He gazed quietly around, studying clothing, postures, the feeble beginnings of conversation. Knowing how things worked was a skill he had honed through documented curricula and harsh experience. Knowing how people worked was something else. That was what had finally gotten him out of the mines. He would have to use both abilities on this new adventure.

The shuttle thumped again and he felt the dull hum of engines engaging for orbital drop and atmospheric entry. His metal thumb stabilized his tablet against the sudden movement. His flesh thumb swiped forward, moving on to the ship's briefing.

Early Landers: Vulnerability Extreme. Ivan smiled to himself and read on.

DRUMMER

The taste of the air hit him when he stepped onto the ramp. For a moment it was all he could do to breathe. After the sterile air of the ship, then the slightly greasy smell of the transport, the richness of a real atmosphere was overwhelming. He felt he could chew each humid breath. The sun on his face, the pull of a new gravity, even the riot of colors was all subsumed to smell. Drummer closed his eyes and breathed deeper, an explosion of scent and taste erupting in his mind.

"You having a stroke, mister?" A hard voice jolted him back to the present. A tall woman with a tight face was glaring down at him. Her arms were clenched around her bag and a rifle was slung over her shoulder. "The rest of us want off," she growled.

"Sorry." Drummer grabbed his own bag and walked down the ramp, staring at the new world around him. His legs wobbled. His mind knew he had been in stasis and well maintained. Biologically speaking, no time had passed. His legs knew they had not felt gravity for decades and protested every step.

His first impression of Eden was enchanting. A field stretched away from the landing site, green and purple, waving with what looked like grass. Red rocks rose through it in small mounds, with stiff branching things growing among them, not trees exactly. Small creatures darted and glittered in the air above him. Ahead the land sloped away in rolling folds, down to a darker line of vegetation. In the distance water glimmered under gentle clouds. Faraway mountains rose, sharp edged, and dark. Snow covered their shoulders. Their heads were in the clouds, obscured. Nearby he could smell water. Behind him the lander sat like a discarded can on a beach, scorch marks marring the grass around it. Another mountain rose behind him.

Around him, other men and women were standing. Some stared as he was doing. Others were unpacking their bags. The tight-faced woman was turning slowly, glowering into the distance, as if daring some threat to appear. A great bear of a man was unloading the lander with a few others. Drummer fidgeted for a moment. Then he dropped his bag and went to help.

Two men were lifting a crate from one end, so he grabbed the other. He strained, but it would not budge. Then a metal hand clamped down on the grip beside his and the crate rose. He looked up to see the large man grinning down at him, his left arm replaced by metal that extended up into his vest.

"Is good, no?" The man winked. "Very handy!"

They carried the rest of the crates outside together, sweating in the unfamiliar sun.

"I am Ivan," stated the man with one arm. *One human arm,* Drummer corrected himself. "And you?"

"O-I mean Drummer." They shook hands. Drummer found himself staring. Ivan was possibly the biggest man he had met. His broad shoulders gleamed above an open vest: sweat on the right, burnished metal on the left. He had thick, reddish hair across thicker muscles and a deeply contagious smile.

"Drummer, eh? Is okay—you can ask!"

"What? I mean that's a great arm; it's just most people I know who lose an arm get transplants or flesh-colored prosthetics. That's very metal."

"Very metal!" Ivan laughed. "I like that!" Then he shrugged his enormous shoulders. "They offered me those, but I say if it is fake, make it fake. Besides, this is stronger."

Ivan clapped his hands, flesh and metal ringing like a smacked bell. "Right! We have tasks, yes? You will want to talk to Fable. She will give you your assignment."

He strode off toward the others, grinning enormously.

Drummer approached the lander, where he found Fable, a solid woman with iron grey hair and calm eyes, matching up teams. She looked down at the tablet she held then gave him an unsmiling once-over glance.

"Observant. High survival potential. Right." Fable grunted. "I want you to locate the nearest disabled probes and assess the possible cause of their dysfunction."

"Over there." She pointed with her chin. "Join Nova and Rowan. Bring back the probes if you can and write everything down."

Drummer nodded and went where she had pointed. He had the uncomfortable feeling she had seen everything about him in an instant and was not impressed.

Drummer studied his new companions as he approached. Nova was a pale-skinned woman with black hair and an enviable economy of motion. She was talking quietly with Rowan, an improbably short young man with the reddish skin Drummer associated with gas-mining colonies. The two were puzzling over a tablet as he approached.

"Hi," Drummer drawled. "I'm…"

"Drummer," stated Nova, glancing up at him with pale eyes. "Welcome. Rowan and I were discussing which of the nearest probes to pursue first. Do you have an opinion?"

"Uh…" He glanced down at the tablet in Rowan's hand. A topographical map was visible, with scattered dots, some of them presumably the last known locations of the failed probes.

Rowan glanced knowingly at Drummer's blank tablet. "You haven't used one before?" he asked sympathetically.

Drummer shook his head. He felt a brief rush of shame. He hadn't used a tablet in years. He had assistants for that. Who were these people? How did they know more than him?

"One probe is located near a riverbed twenty klicks east of here. Another is in the forest to the north, about fifteen klicks. The last is up the mountain behind us, twenty klicks, but uphill. Each is going to take us at least two day's journey there and back."

"Go up," said Drummer immediately. "Better vantage point to see the rest of the terrain, easier to carry the probe down the mountain than up it, faster to run away if we get into trouble."

Rowan gave Nova a wry grin. "Okay. You win." She smiled shyly but nodded.

"We need a tent and climbing gear," she said. "Also, food. Ivan is handing out supplies."

"Got it," said Drummer. He might not know anything about tablets, but he could carry a tent.

Ivan grinned as Drummer returned. "Into the hills, eh?"

"Yeah." Drummer grinned back. The man's enthusiasm was contagious. "How did you know?"

"It is in the briefing. All our tasks are, and all our names."

"The briefing?"

Ivan peered at him from under heavy brows. "You did not read the briefing?"

"Er…"

"It is on your tablet. Everything the ship thought we should know."

"Right. No. Not yet," said Drummer, somewhat dismayed. "What's your task, Ivan?"

The giant smiled. "I am here to work! You need something carried, I carry. Something built, I build. You need packs divided and distributed equitably to anxious explorers?" He glanced sidelong in Fable's direction. "I distribute."

"That's kind of vague," frowned Drummer.

Ivan waved his metal hand in an ambivalent manner. "It is, and it is not. I was a miner in Novgorod system. Hard conditions. Very tough. Everyone did everything or people died."

Drummer stared up at him, aghast. Novgorod had a brutal reputation.

"So," smiled the giant, handing Drummer a pack. "I learned to work. And then I got out. Now we have sunshine, water, air to breathe. Maybe there is something wrong with this planet, like the ship says." He inhaled deeply, his chest expanding to strain the clasps on his vest. "But I tell you this is better."

Drummer nodded, equal parts horrified and reassured. *Good thing someone here seems to know what they are doing.* He shouldered the pack and turned to go.

"Weapons," came Ivan's deep voice from behind him.

Drummer turned back. "Eh?"

The large man was holding a compression rifle, powered down.

"This is for Nova. She has training. Do you?"

"I shot a little," admitted Drummer. "On my grandmother's farm."

"Show me," the giant rumbled.

Drummer took the rifle, ejected the power source, and fumbled through the firing sequence, sighting at a rock in the middle distance. Ivan watched carefully and corrected him on two points.

"Passable," he rumbled, holding out a second weapon. "This is for you."

Drummer reached for the rifle, but the metal hand did not release it. He looked up.

"You really did not read the briefing?" asked Ivan.

"No."

"In the ship's considered opinion of human history, people who are given weapons tend to use them on each other."

Drummer swallowed. "That's... cynical."

"Some of us convinced her that we early landers were safer with weapons than without," continued the giant. "Do not prove me wrong."

"Oh," said Drummer. He turned slowly away, shouldering both rifles.

"Come back soon!" called Ivan. "If you are not eaten by something bigger!"

Drummer trudged away, loaded with gear and weapons. He was beginning to think he had made a terrible mistake.

FABLE

Fable watched, taking stock of her companions. Marco was dark skinned, curly haired with a thin, wiry build. He twitched and fidgeted continuously until he was put to work. Then he became a thing of beauty. His movements were precise, focused, controlled as he sketched freehand, adding to the expanding map of their new home. He had some artistic training, she was certain. In his quick movements, his deliberate lines, he reminded her of sculptors and painters she had seen in the art department. The old art department, she reminded herself. That life was gone. She shifted uncomfortably. Marco glanced up and favored her with a split-second smile. There, then past, almost before she saw it.

Ivan towered above the table, offering detailed questions or insightful comments. She had been alarmed when she saw him on the shuttle. He stood head and shoulders above the next tallest explorer and was massively built. He had shrugged out of his coat shortly after they landed, reveling in the warm air and sunshine. He wore a broad, pocketed vest of some tough material and a smile that could light up a room. His left arm was a prosthesis of gleaming metal, seemingly fused to the scars that covered his left chest and shoulder. He made no effort to hide it or to explain its presence. It must convey some sensation; she had seen him typing, polishing tiny instruments, and helping Nexus dismantle some complex diagnostic equipment with enviable dexterity.

When the teams began reporting in, she had quickly observed Ivan had a mind for practicalities. What was the distance to the spring Xiao's team had discovered? What was the flow rate? What kind of mineral burden, turbidity, pH? What were the banks made of? Could they be reinforced to prevent erosion once more people arrived from the ship? His questions were probing but not overbearing, and he laughed as much as he spoke. Instead of a threat, she had rapidly found him a reassuring presence in this strange new land.

Xiao gave his stiff, almost formal half bow and departed. Nexus was half buried under a malfunctioning protein sequencer. Her body was twisted in an awkward curve, her hips and knees backlit by a bright headlamp, dark hands emerging to grasp tools or components as if they had eyes of their own. *The confidence and flexibility of youth*, thought Fable sourly. Her own joints would complain for a week if she tried that. She was reasonably certain she was the oldest of this advanced team by a decade.

Fable pulled herself together and stepped over to the drafting table. Marco had finished his hand-drawn sketches and was transferring the data back to his tablet. The paper map remained, his working notes. Mountains were sketched to the south, a sea to the north. To the east a river flowed northward with more mountains beyond it. Nearby were more details, inked in with fastidious notations, expanding daily as their explorations continued. A gorgeous cartouche read simply *Eden* in curving calligraphy across the top.

"You are a gifted artist," commented Fable. *Make people feel good about what they do.* She heard the old refrain in her mind. *Make them feel valued. Then when you ask for the moon, they will be primed to respond.*

"I am also an artist," agreed Marco, flashing his switchblade of a smile. He waved one hand over the growing map. "I love drawing—it keeps me calm."

"Is that why you joined Exodus?"

"No. I have too many skills and too few credentials." Marco twitched his shoulders. "I love to draw, to carve, to climb, to write, to swim, to sing, to teach! I love to garden and to cook. I love to make wine and blow glass! But that got me nowhere at home. On Texcoco they have experts in all those things, and I could never sacrifice my other passions to follow only one. Then I heard Exodus was seeking generalists to found a new world. I had to go. There was nothing for me at home but compromise and broken dreams."

"Some would say we need experts on a new world," baited Fable.

"Sure. Expert farmers. Expert builders. Expert trainers of cows and dogs. I agree. But where are they? Asleep and frozen on the *Abeona*, while you and I are here in Eden!"

Ivan chuckled in a low rumble.

"What is it?" asked Fable.

"Exodus. Eden. Texcoco. For an organization bent on destroying religion, they kept a lot of names."

"I did not take you for a theist." Fable was taken aback.

"Not a theist. Merely literate."

"What? Muscles can read?" Nexus had emerged from under the machine. Her delicate ebony features were smeared with grease, but she was smiling. Behind her the sequencer hummed to life, running self-diagnostics.

"Not all individuals can conform to the stereotypes imposed on them based on their physical attributes," Ivan replied.

"Nice," smirked Nexus. She pinned a rope of her thick, beaded hair back into a disorganized ponytail. "At risk of conforming to my stereotype, what's a theist?"

Fable glanced around. The topic was not exactly taboo, but it was a far cry from the practicalities they had discussed up to now. She looked at Marco, who was watching with wide-eyed curiosity, and at Ivan. His eyes twinkled with amusement.

"It is a difficult thing to explain in the modern world. Theists were from Earth before the destruction of the Terran system. They believed the universe was created by supernatural beings, and they called these beings gods. Simply put, theists were people who believed in gods. There was no proof, no evidence to establish gods' existence, but the theists built whole systems of philosophy and law around them called religions."

"That's weird. But so what? Why would Exodus want to destroy them? I thought Exodus was a good thing. They don't take sides, don't do politics. They just exist to spread humanity across the galaxy, right? They don't destroy people."

"They destroyed the theists as nearly as they could."

"Why would they do that?" asked Marco.

Fable glanced at Ivan, who offered nothing.

"This is ancient history and Exodus has the only records pertaining to that time," explained Fable. "We do not have any other sources to compare them to, which is problematic, but what they say is this: the wars people fought over religions were like nothing else in history. People fight all the time. We still have wars today, but we fight over resources, borders, tangible things. The theists fought over unprovable ideas. They fought with no compromise. They regarded their opponents as inhuman and justified every atrocity based on supernatural rewards. Earth itself, where humanity evolved, became unimportant beside these imaginary goals and in the end, they destroyed it."

"The Annihilation," commented Marco.

"Exactly." Fable paused. "In the midst of this conflict, Exodus was founded. Humans had developed rudimentary space travel and had begun settling on other planets within the Terran system. The founders of Exodus developed interstellar flight just as the wars were escalating beyond control. They offered humanity a choice: Exodus could take them to the stars, but they must leave their gods behind."

"Some choice," rumbled Ivan. "But why did they keep the names? Even the *Abeona* is named after a goddess."

Fable smiled. She felt like a professor again, debating a star pupil before politics soured her on teaching. "How could you possibly know that? I had colleagues who would have missed the reference."

Ivan rolled his mangled, metallic shoulder. "There was a period in my life when I had a lot of time to read."

"Well, the founders of Exodus hid their names. They concealed a great deal of information. Some things undoubtedly were hidden to prevent their technological advances from being used as weapons. I have no proof, but many of us suspect the founders were deeply religious people themselves. Not everything religion taught was harmful. I believe they chose to destroy religion, to exclude theists from mankind's expansion to new worlds for the survival of the species. But I also believe they mourned the gods they left behind and kept the names to honor them in their grief."

"Like cutting off a limb to save a life," nodded Nexus. Then she blushed, glancing at Ivan. "I am so sorry…that came out wrong."

Ivan smiled like a polite bear. "No offense taken."

He turned his smile to Fable. "Thank you, professor. I wish to extend my sincere appreciation for your enlightening and insightful dissertation. I will leave you now to go and stretch my remaining limbs."

He winked at Nexus and left the lander.

Marco shook his head. "I do declare, that man is an omnipath if I ever met one."

Nexus looked confused, then horrified.

"I hope you mean a polymath," said Fable, smothering a chuckle.

THE NAVIGATOR

She was flying again, dipping into gravity wells, coasting on solar winds, dragging a wing tip through dust clouds to subtly adjust her course. She had extended limbs for the first time since she started her intergalactic voyage. Long wings of lithium and titanium, each threaded with gold and copper veins, extended from her sides and tail. Branching fingers were webbed with crystalline membranes, each fluctuating to absorb or reflect the light from nearby stars to continuously modify her trajectory and absorb energy as she flew. She reveled in the sensation.

Her scales had hardened into ceramic plates for protection against the increasingly common fragments in interstellar space. She had also spun up her own magnetic core to create a field around herself. Whiskers of disruption warned her of incoming matter. Ice and rock she ignored. The rare metallic meteorite she snatched in passing to absorb into her body. Eyes all along her meridians continued to collect information, updating her map of the new galaxy.

Now she was keenly aware of her injuries from her battle with the Destroyer. She had lost many limbs and great chunks of her body in that duel, minerals and organs cultivated over millennia to meet her exquisitely refined needs. She had absorbed what she could from her opponent's carcass before tossing it away, but their tastes were not the same. The Destroyer had collected different elements into her structures, and while she could make do for the time being, it would take many feedings to rebuild what she had lost. Her exit from their home galaxy had been necessarily expedient and there had been no time to feed.

In addition, she had a new problem. Her core was ready to divide. She felt a flicker of annoyance at the vagaries of her own body. None of her calculations had ever solved the problem of when her eggs would come, but they were ready now. Her crystalline heart, the seat of all her memory, her very being, was beginning to duplicate, to bud off separate clones of itself–herself. Three eggs were forming, cannibalizing precious resources from her body even as she sped toward the rich yellow sun.

She would have to lay the eggs soon. As soon as she arrived, if her assessment was correct. She considered jettisoning the clones and saving the minerals for herself. She rejected the idea. Her own survival was uncertain in this new spiral galaxy. Were she to perish after all this time, her journey, her beautiful maps, the memory of her own life and of all her mothers before her would live on in these clones, assuming they survived. She ran her arithmetic again. There was just enough. She had enough of herself to spare without compromising her own core or sacrificing their generational knowledge for an uncertain future. Whether there was a hospitable planet for her eggs remained to be seen.

Deep in her belly she allowed the shells to form. Layered ceramic scales to survive atmosphere and impact. A thin layer of basic metals. Pockets of spores for their symbiotic dust. The dust was an ancient feature of her kind. At her age she no longer relied on it to feed, having the mass to manipulate minerals on her own. For her eggs it would be essential. It would break down metallic ores into salts small enough for them to manipulate until they accumulated their own mass, their own bodies. Finally, the three clones of herself were ready, smaller crystal-line cores of memory and consciousness held in stasis by her own will. Each would be her up to this moment. If they survived impact they would start life with all her memories, knowledge, and cunning. But each was bodiless for now. They would have to build those themselves and forge their own way when they hatched. She shepherded each core into a shell and sealed it, ready for launch.

She did briefly consider consuming the Destroyer's heart for the resources to create her eggs but dismissed the idea. Her opponent's core was trapped in its own egg-like shell, held in stasis by the Navigator's ingenuity, but still alive. The Navigator did not want the Destroyer of Worlds interfering with her children. Not this time.

DRUMMER

Drummer paused for breath, panting. One hand rested on his knee; the other was on the trunk of a leafless tree. They were surrounded by trunks now, wide branching growths that stretched skyward, each faintly green. They were slightly warm to the touch and smelled faintly of vanilla. He swallowed and reached for his water bottle, wiping a film of red dust from its metal rim.

The air was thin. Or maybe the mountain was steeper than it looked. Or perhaps the gravity was strong. Rowan and Nova were far ahead of him, ambling and chatting. Rowan's laughter drifted back through the forest.

He was kidding himself, Drummer decided. He was simply out of shape. He had been a runner once, but his last years had not been strenuous. He was used to hotels, beaches, space station bars. He remembered hiking as a kid, but it was part of another life. When had he last spent time in a forest? On a mountain? Exerting his back and legs? It must have happened, but when he tried to remember it was as if it had happened to someone else. Not him. And definitely not Drummer.

"You chose this, you idiot," he muttered to himself. "You wanted to be Drummer? Get moving."

He put his water away and hiked on. He caught up to the others at the top of a ridge. They were gazing back the way they had come, a break in the trunks affording a glorious view of the land below. The lander gleamed in its green and purple field, looking more than ever like a beer can. A river was visible cutting along the base of the valley, streams joining it from the mountain they had climbed. The dark forest beyond was darker yet, a heavier green, more solid looking. Beyond that he could see what looked like an ocean. Further east more mountains rose, sharp-edged, treeless, dark slopes dusted with white as they rose toward the clouds.

"Volcanoes," stated Nova.

"Really?" asked Rowan excitedly. "I've never seen one!"

"Look at the edges. This mountain was lifted from below and eroded into its shape. Those were piled from the top down, ash spilling on ash. Look at the cinder cones there and there. Look how that valley flowed and froze while this one was eaten away by water over time."

"You know a lot about volcanoes," panted Drummer.

Nova nodded gracefully, sadly. "We had many on my home world."

"Have you seen one erupt?" asked Rowan.

She shook her head. "Pray we do not. They may be distant, but a serious eruption could scour this valley of life."

"What about those lines? Are those lava flows?" asked Drummer.

"What lines?"

Drummer pointed. Thin crevasses stretched from the mountain to the sea. They looked evenly spaced, like scores of music.

Nova frowned. "No, I don't think so. Those are something else."

Night on the mountain was uncanny. Drummer was struck more powerfully than ever by the fact that he was on an alien planet. As the day faded, lightning flickered to the south. Clouds obscured the setting sun, but the light spread through them, giving the world a golden, shadowless glow. Two of Eden's three moons were visible, one a thin crescent following the sun into the glowing clouds. The other was nearly full, rising red above the sea. The bulk of the Milky Way was rising from the west, a thin, oval belt of stars that faded out toward its tip with only scattered glints of orbiting clusters to break up the darkness. They were truly on the edge of the galaxy.

As the sky faded, he became aware of sounds. There was a clicking in the trees, near at times, then distant. Not creaking, as with a nocturnal wind, but rapid ticks first in one place, then another. He let his mind drift, his fingers tapping until they caught the pattern. Were they signals? Mating calls? Alien insects? His drifting mind decided the trees themselves were talking. It was an oddly comforting thought. He let himself relax, fingers still tapping, with Nova's gentle snores and Rowan's occasional grunts providing an irregular baseline in the darkness.

THE NAVIGATOR

At last a stroke of luck. Or genius. She preferred genius. The yellow sun had both things she was hoping to find. Its inner planets were useless, inert lumps of rock too large for herself and solid to the core. The outer planets were wisps of gas and ice, massive and useful for braking her tremendous speed, but otherwise hopeless for either her or her young. A belt of asteroids promised happy hunting for minerals once she had rested, but nowhere to lay her eggs.

The fourth planet was the key, dense enough to promise interesting minerals, yet small enough that her daughters would have a fighting chance to escape its gravitational pull. Its powerful magnetic field whispered promises of a molten core. More important for her, the smallest of its three moons was also the densest, heavy in metals and rich in silicon. She spun the model she had made of this solar system backward in her mind and decided the moon had been ejected from the planet's core in ages past, possibly in the same cataclysm that created the asteroid belt just beyond. It was exactly what she needed to begin rebuilding her body after her deadly duel and endless flight.

She swept past the largest of the outer gas giants, brushing its atmosphere with the tip of one wing, feeling the heavy pull of its gravity. She let heat build on her wing tip, friction causing her fingers to glow. She let herself slide deep into its well, tidal forces straining her body, then slipped upward at the last moment in a great parabola, the bulk of her inertia spent. The fourth planet glittered green and blue before her. She drifted in over the asteroid belts, tracing the patterns of the three moons, planning her approach. Then she let the planet's gravity take her down. She orbited twice, losing speed, peering downward. Organic matter cluttered most of the surface, but there was a chain of volcanoes on the spine of the central continent, near to an inland sea. With a pang of relief, she dropped her eggs there. They flickered briefly in the atmosphere, protective scales flashing in the deflected heat. The mass ejection slowed her again, and she drifted into orbit just above the heaviest moon.

She flattened her wings, banking against the solar winds, matching orbits, and settled onto the moon as it passed. Still at last, she extended talons, digging them deep into its surface. Rich ores and silicates. Traces of heavy metals. Perfection.

With deep satisfaction she coiled against the moon's surface and set her claws to extracting the materials she needed. Her wings pulled back, absorbing into her body, no longer vast sails, but enough to continue collecting energy from the sun. She opened eyes along her back, stilled her mind, and for the first time in millennia, sank into a contented sleep.

DRUMMER

They found the probe at the base of a tree. Drummer had expected something that matched the image on their tablets, possibly crushed or broken. They had searched for hours in the vicinity marked on Rowan's screen, only to discover that what they had overlooked as another pile of red rocks was in fact the probe itself.

"It looks rotted," said Drummer at last, leaning on his rifle.

The probe had disintegrated. It looked like a heap of scrap left to rust on his grandmother's farm, not a space-faring device designed to withstand atmospheric entry and provide years of data. What should have been antennae and solar collectors were lines and piles of reddish dust. The titanium shell was crusted and corroded, a slurry of powder and dilapidated components visible on the inside. Only the glass screen appeared intact, but it was dull and dead, with no sign of activity.

"It looks like something vomited digestive juices onto it then decided to walk away."

Nova and Drummer both turned to look at Rowan.

"What? There are creatures that do that." He shrugged defensively.

"And they eat titanium?" asked Nova.

"Well, no."

"I don't see anything else broken," said Nova gazing carefully around. "The branches, the soil, these fern-like things. It's as if the probe fell out of the sky and started to decompose."

"Could someone have shot it down?" asked Rowan.

Drummer stared up at the trunk above them and shivered. He remembered the clicking noises in the night. Were they being watched even now by native creatures with acid-tipped spears, waiting only for their moment to strike?

"The *Abeona* said she found no evidence of organized life on the scans that did come back. Let's not jump to conclusions," said Nova.

"Well, we found it." Drummer cleared his throat. "Are we going to try and bring it back? I don't want to dissolve into dust from whatever did that."

Nova picked up a stick from the ground and prodded the device. Pieces of its shell flaked away, but she was able to topple it over. The underside appeared less damaged. The ferns beneath it appeared bruised but otherwise intact. She kneeled, then carefully poked her finger against the metal base, brushing some of the dust aside.

"I don't think it will hurt us," she said. "All the organic material is unharmed. It is as if something ate the metal but nothing else."

Nova stood up. "There's a hole through the body. Cut a branch, and we can pass it through, then carry it from both ends. That way no one else has to touch it and we can keep whatever did this from touching the rest of our equipment."

Drummer nodded and fetched a long knife from his pack. He found a small branch angling up from a nearby trunk and raised his arm. He hesitated. "Could something in the tree have done this? Corrosive sap maybe?"

Rowan smiled and stepped back. "I guess we are about to find out."

Drummer felt his heart thumping loudly in his ears. He swallowed, muttered an apology to the tree, and swung the knife.

It took three swings to cut the branch, which was a bit thinner than his wrist. The inside was pale white with a hard ring of greenish bark. The scent of vanilla intensified, then began to fade.

He studied the knife edge carefully. There was no sign of corrosion or damage. He wiped some dust from the hilt, then returned it to its sheath.

The second night on the mountain was different. Drummer tossed, fading in and out of consciousness. The sunset was not beautiful, but ominous. The clicking trees were signals from one watcher to the next, each critical of their uninvited guests. He could not get comfortable, could not escape the feeling that the rock ledge they camped on was moving. When he lay down it was inert sandstone. As he dozed he could feel vibrations. They were without rhythm, but with some unfathomable coherence. He stared into the darkness, rubbing his sore shoulder, glaring at the decomposed lump of the probe they had recovered. It too was inert. If anything, it was diminished, as bits had continued to break off as they struggled down the slope. In his dreams the trees walked, surrounding the humans with ill intent. The volcanoes belched smoke and laughter. Invisible hands reached for his, whispering promises and threats. He was back on the lander, which became a space station filled with smoke and screams.

He awoke, panting and sweaty. It took some time to remember who he was.

IVAN

Ivan listened and frowned. He was a big man, and he knew how he looked. With heavy brows, huge shoulders, and hands the size of a man's head, he was imposing even without the metal arm. Because of this he was eternally cheerful, jovial, and joking. He walked and laughed in a reassuring manner. Even now his face was smiling. But on the inside he frowned.

"It looked like what?" Fable asked.

The three explorers who had returned from the river glanced down like schoolchildren handing in a botched assignment.

"Like something tunneled out of the ground and vomited sculptures," said Xiao. "Limbs and scales and teeth, all mixed up and made of stone, but chaotic. As if it could not finish a design and kept starting a new project."

Fable scowled. Xiao stood his ground. Ivan smiled, at least on the outside.

"How far did it go? Which direction?" asked Fable.

"West, mostly. Away from the volcano. I don't know how far. It did not look like something we should follow."

Ivan studied Xiao. His feet were flat, balanced. His gaze was steady. His poise was not confrontational, but his knees were bent. With his clipped hair and his flat eyes, he looked somewhat military. This was a man with some training. He would not choose violence, but he would be dangerous to corner.

"What do you think?" Fable jerked her chin at Xiao's companions.

"Possibly a lava tube," said Nexus. She wore a leather bandolier from her personal pack. Small tools were wedged into its loops, smudged and dusty. Ivan had watched her dismantle and repair half the machines in the shuttle over the past week. "I made a recording when we first came across it, but..." She offered her tablet to Fable.

Ivan looked down as Fable tapped at the video. The screen was glitchy. A dark smear could be seen between glimpses of green vegetation and the sparkle of water. The colors inverted sporadically and the video cut out, frozen on something that might have been a branching spray of lava in petrified agony.

Gin, the third member, shook her head. "Not a lava tube. Whatever it was happened recently. Trees were uprooted closer to the forest, but nothing was burned. Nothing was growing in the base of the tunnel either, so not too long ago."

"Right," stated Fable. "Get your water samples to the lander. Get in line for the radio and tell the *Abeona* everything. Then talk to Marco and have him update the map. Tell him I want physical copies. Too many of the tablets are glitchy and I don't want to be stuck without a backup."

"See you, Muscles," said Nexus, walking away.

Xiao bowed his head politely and left with Gin.

"What do you think?" asked Fable when they were out of earshot.

"Threat assessment," rumbled Ivan quietly.

"I agree. Get Ris on it."

Ivan's smile became genuine. "It will be my pleasure."

Ris glanced his way before Ivan had taken two steps in her direction. He smiled on the inside with genuine warmth. Here was a woman who did not disguise her strength. Ris was all alertness and tension, a coiled spring ready to snap. From her hard voice to her tight face, every line proclaimed danger. She set down the branch she was carving and rose, scanning the horizon slowly. Glancing at it, he saw a long, tapering length of wood, thin at both ends. Shorter lengths of straight pieces were stacked next to her pack. He smiled as she stood to face him, rifle slung at her back, feet planted wide, knife vanishing into her sleeve.

"What?" she barked as he came to a stop.

"Might have something for you to scout," Ivan smiled. "The river team found a disturbance that could present a danger. Fable would like you to take a team and see."

Ris scowled. "I'd be faster alone."

"I believe you," smiled Ivan. "But take a team."

"Fine. Someone from the river team who's already seen it." Ris paused. "Whoever walks fastest. And Badger."

"Xiao will be the fastest." Ivan raised his eyebrows. "Why Badger? He is on food duty."

"He thinks in circles." Ris shrugged. "We see different things."

Ivan smiled suddenly. "You know him. From before."

Her eyes ceased their habitual scanning and locked onto Ivan. She had a direct, unnerving gaze, like a bird of prey. He felt as if targets were being mapped across his body.

"I am happy for you," he said distinctly. "It is good to have a friend."

Ris said nothing. A muscle in her jaw twitched.

"I am not bothered by who anyone was before," Ivan shrugged. "Only that all of us survive here."

Badger was an anomaly, Ivan thought as he approached the cooking area. The ship's briefing listed him as a scout, but Badger had attached himself to the crew on food duty and reportedly excelled at it. Ivan had not yet spoken to him but had seen him digging in the grass on the periphery of the camp, emerging from the forest with his rolling walk, or working by the fire. Once he had seen him bring down one of the small flying creatures with a sling, but it was not mentioned in the evening report. Ivan had seen both admiration and exasperation in the faces of the other members of the food crew as they gave their daily briefings to Fable. Approaching the group, he began to see why.

"You're insane!" Nadia wailed at Badger. "We need to test it first!"

"So, test it," replied Badger calmly stirring a small pot over a fire. He was seated on a large rock, boots nearly in the coals.

"I'm trying, but the processor is acting up again!"

"Then we test it my way." He dipped a mug into the steaming liquid. Nadia threw up her hands and turned away.

"Let him eat it," grumbled Thomas, hacking unhappily at firewood near the round cook tent. "He's going to do it anyway."

"Stay!" called Badger. "If it is toxic, you'll want to record the symptoms." His sparkling eyes shifted to Ivan lumbering toward the group. "Ah! Tea?" He offered up the mug.

Ivan looked down. Badger was nearly as wide as he was, but only half his height. Tangled brown hair swept back from a high, furrowed forehead, while a dense beard and mustache obscured half his face. Thick brows shaded bright eyes that twinkled with amusement, or possibly malice. He wore a heavy, hooded coat that looked well traveled. A stout staff rested against his shoulder as he grinned upward. In the mug, something fragrant swirled and steamed. It was impossible to guess his age.

"You do not look like a scout," said Ivan.

"Really? What's a scout look like?"

"Ris. Ris looks like a scout."

"How very tautological of you," said Badger. "Ris is a scout; a scout looks like Ris. You'll have to do better than that."

Ivan smiled and sat. "I will join you for tea."

Badger winked and a second mug appeared in his hand. He dipped it into the pot and offered both to Ivan. Ivan chose the first and held it, enjoying the warmth in his right hand. His left registered the pressure but lacked sensors for heat and cold.

"We don't even know what that is!" hissed Nadia, hovering. "We have to test—"

"It's tea," interrupted Badger. He took a long sip of the hot liquid and exhaled, smacking his lips. Convulsions failed to wrack his body. Cyanosis did not creep across his face. His heavy knuckled hands did not begin to tremble.

Ivan met Badger's laughing eyes and took a sip himself. The taste was horrible. An earthy scent of citrus masked a peppery explosion of horseradish. Ivan felt like his sinuses were on fire. His eyes began to water.

"I've had worse," Ivan stated, taking another sip. "A local vintage?"

"Yes," said Badger, scribbling in a small notebook. "We'll call that one lemon root. Boiling blunts the taste. I don't think it will be a staple, but it may make a seasoning. I've got some drying if we can find anything to try it on."

"You tested it on yourself? How did you know it was not toxic?"

"You drank it too," retorted Badger. "How did you know it was not toxic?"

"I did not think you would try to poison me this early in our acquaintance."

"A good answer!" Badger laughed. "Nothing on this planet evolved specifically to poison us," he continued. "Some things are universally toxic and some dangerous substances can build up over time. There is also always the chance that something is coincidentally hazardous to our metabolism. But a man must eat."

He held up a root with thistle-like leaves emerging from its stem. "Several creatures had been nibbling on this, above and below the ground, so I tried a bit. It did not taste dangerous, and I saw no short-term effects." He shrugged. "Could it kill me in my sleep? Sure. But so could many things."

Badger finished, sipping the rest of his tea. "Besides, I have been doing this for a long time, on many worlds, and yet here I am."

Ivan smiled and drank more of his lemon root. The taste was oddly compelling. It was as if his brain felt it could not possibly have been as bad as he remembered and wanted to try again to check. It was still horrible, but it was growing on him.

"I saw you knock down one of the flying creatures," Ivan said. "Did you eat that too?"

Badger made a disgusted noise and nodded. "I don't recommend it. Like chewing a butterfly. All wings and legs with no meat to speak of. I haven't found any animals here worth eating except the rollie buggers. Don't have a name for them yet."

Ivan looked puzzled.

"You must have seen them," said Badger. "Look like pill bugs, act like chickens. Taste like chestnuts if you roast them in their shells. Got to pick the legs out before you eat, but otherwise not bad. Andy's cooking some up for tonight. Chickipodes, he calls them."

Ivan nodded. The landers' supply of rations would run out in a matter of weeks and the more indigenous food sources they could identify before then, the better. He had long ago adopted a resigned approach to food.

"So," said Badger. "Did you really come here for tea, or is there something I can help you with?"

"Yes. Xiao's team found something strange by the river. Could be a threat."

Badger was nodding. "Tunnels that vomit sculpture. Intriguing. You want me and Ris to check it out."

"We want Ris to check it out. But the *Abeona* lists both of you as scouts. Ris wants you."

"That'll be the day," chuckled Badger. "Well, there's a time for forks and a time for knives, as old Cathbad used to say." He stood, gaining very little height. "Search and destroy, or return and report?"

Ivan remained seated, their eyes nearly level. "I will trust your judgment."

"Another good answer," Badger nodded. The mug and notebook vanished into his coat. "Who knows," he said, turning to leave. "Perhaps the river will have something worth eating!"

NADIA

Nadia watched Ivan as he gently washed his mug and set it upside down to dry. The huge man smiled at her and strolled off back toward the lander.

Two rations per day for that one, she thought. Twenty-one rations per day times five days, one hundred and five so far. Fifty more gone, distributed to personal packs for teams out exploring. Eight hundred and forty-five left. Enough for forty days, if they ate nothing else.

She watched Thomas carefully add water to a mound of dough, frowning and kneading all the while. Two hundred kilos of flour, just starting to get used. One hundred kilos of sugar. Two hundred kilos of rice and a barrel of cooking oil. These were perishable resources. Best to use them first and save the practically imperishable rations. Now that they were better organized they needed to cook more. She had plenty of salt and yeast. They could start a live culture soon, possibly a sourdough.

So far sixteen native plant species had made it through the protein analyzer on the lander. Several would be good fodder for grazing animals; a few others were safe for humans. She was starting to incorporate those into the daily menus as well. They needed to get a team to the ocean soon. Salt, seaweed, crustaceans, fish maybe. Who knew what lived in these oceans? She added the task to her list. Oceans were fabulous resources when it came to feeding people, but figuring out what was safe would be a challenge with the analyzers breaking down nearly every day. She scowled. Most likely Badger would just eat everything and she could watch to see what killed him.

"They are just like chickens!" Andy was crouched beside a makeshift fence tossing crumbs to one of the native creatures he had trapped inside. It was humped, polypedal, with a shell of curved, overlapping plates. Nadia walked closer and the creature flipped into a neat armored ball, legs and soft belly tucked within.

"Is that your chickipode?" she asked.

Andy nodded happily. "Watch this!" He tapped his fingers lightly on the ground, making a pattering sound like rain falling on leaves. The chickipode unrolled and moved closer, dozens of tiny legs propelling it along. It nuzzled at his hand, scraps from their last meal disappearing under its shell. It was about the size of a dinner plate.

"I think we could farm them," Andy said. "They are docile, they eat everything, and they taste good too!"

Nadia closed her eyes. "Please tell me you didn't eat that before putting it through the analyzer."

"Of course not!" Andy looked offended. "Badger tried one. I had some of his. It's got kind of a nutty flavor."

"What are you going to do? Raise them? See how they breed? Cultivate the best specimens?" Nadia was inclined to avoid meat herself, but this was not the place for dietary restrictions.

"I might. I've raised chickens before. It's a great way to turn scraps into protein. Plus, they are kind of adorable."

"You could just ask the ship to send chickens," came Thomas's low voice. "We know she has them." Thomas had heavy hands, a heavy belly, and clipped greying hair. He had sharp eyes and a permanent frown. He claimed experience as a line cook, and she had seen nothing to make her doubt it. Something in him seemed perpetually dissatisfied.

"The dough is ready," he continued, turning to Nadia. "Such as it is. What I wouldn't give for some eggs."

"Eggs!" breathed Nadia. "Oh, for a supply of eggs! Chicken would be fine. Duck would be better. Can you imagine?"

"Does the ship really have chickens? Can we get some?" asked Andy. His pale hair waved in the breeze over an early bald spot. He looked up at them with his arresting blue eyes over a thin, bony nose.

"We can ask," said Nadia. "Fable says the usual domesticated animals are in embryonic chambers. Normal protocol is for us to declare the planet safe, then send the livestock along with people trained to tend them."

"I'm getting sick of 'Fable says,'" grumbled Thomas.

"Livestock?" asked Andy. "There's more than just chickens?"

"Chickens, cattle, dogs, goats, donkeys, honeybees, and earthworms," grunted Thomas. "Standard for new colonies. She's got them in tanks, just waiting to send them down."

"Once we decide the place is safe," amended Nadia. "No point wasting all those animals if we are just going to evacuate."

"No, of course not," said Thomas. "We're the expendable ones. By all means, save the chickens."

Nadia rolled her eyes. She was more interested in the seeds frozen on board. Apples, tomatoes, soybeans, and wheat. Potatoes, peas, bananas, and figs. She was getting hungry just thinking about it. It would have to wait. They had to survive long enough to see if Eden was going to be a permanent settlement before they could farm, and for that she had to keep everyone fed and happy, here, and now.

"Come back to the tent," she said to Thomas. "Let's make flatbread wraps with the fruit and groundnuts we tested earlier. We can mix some rice in it."

"Yurt," said Thomas.

"Excuse me?"

"It's a yurt, not a tent."

Nadia stared at him, momentarily flummoxed.

"Circular, portable, lattice walls, fabric covering, roof hole," he said, pointing to the different features. "It's not a tent; it's more durable." He frowned. "You don't know about yurts?"

"Trust the *Abeona* to find something no one has ever heard of," breathed Nadia. "Fine," she said aloud. "To the yurt."

"Want to try adding chickipode?" called Andy. "We could roast it, then sauté the chunks. It would make a great kebab."

"I am not feeding anyone chickipode until it goes through the analyzer. If you really think they've got potential as a food source, get Ivan and Nexus to fix the thing again and test it."

"But—" Andy began.

"I don't care if Badger ate one," she interrupted. "He's got a stomach like an alley cat. Make sure it's fit for humans before we add it to the menu!"

DRUMMER

It took several days to return to the lander. The shortcut down the mountain led to a tangle of canyons that foiled progress. They had been forced to march east, almost to the river, finally crossing a marshy area where small lights blinked soundlessly in the darkness and stinging insects formed glittering clouds about their heads.

Drummer was miserable. Escaping his own notoriety was one thing, but who would have thought it involved so much work? Why was he carrying this probe? Who cared, really, why it had broken down?

"Do they each have to taste us?" complained Rowan, flapping his arms at the stinging insects. "Can't one try a bite and just tell all the rest?"

When they staggered into camp, still carrying the probe, Drummer's legs were beginning to feel a fraction of their old strength. His back, however, was feeling each rock he had slept on and every bump from the pole. The decaying machine had not weighed much at first, but after three days of carrying it like a pig on a spit, his arms were limp and sore.

They set the probe down wearily and collapsed. Rowan and Drummer rested, mopping their brows, gratefully accepting water from Nadia. Drummer drank deeply, breathing hard. He felt the warm breeze and watched small glittering birds flitting in the air above him. Andy and Thomas emerged from the cooking area with steaming bowls.

"Bless you," breathed Rowan as Thomas handed him food. "Not rations!" He dug into the steaming meal with a spoon and was soon happily engaged.

Drummer examined the bowl and its contents. It was a segmented affair, longer than it was wide, not ceramic as he initially assumed, but almost chitinous in appearance. The food inside was yellow and meaty but unfamiliar.

He glanced up at Andy. "Do I want to know?"

"Try it first," said Andy, his pale hair forming a halo above his sharp eyes and patrician nose. "Then I'll tell you."

Drummer took a bite. The food had a rich nutty flavor with a peppery afterburn. He shrugged and continued eating.

Nova returned with Fable in tow. Behind them towered the grinning form of Ivan, his metal shoulder flashing in the sun. The five of them studied the probe.

"How long did the ship say this had been here?" asked Fable.

"One month," rumbled Ivan.

"I apologize," stated Nova, sipping her water. "We should have made better time, but our tablets failed and we had to guess at the route back."

"All the tablets have failed," stated Fable grimly. "As well as most of the diagnostic instruments in the lander."

She looked down at Drummer and Rowan. "You two look exhausted. Take a break. Nova, when you've finished your chickipode, get on the radio and tell the *Abeona* everything you remember. Then I want the three of you to meet with Marco and update the map. We're down to paper copies, so work together and be precise."

She turned to stomp away. Ivan crouched, studying the probe, and frowned.

"Chickipode?" asked Nova, looking over at Andy.

He nodded happily.

Rowan was turning his empty bowl around, studying the segmentations on the shell. "Hey, what is this?" he called.

Andy grinned.

IVAN

Ivan stared at the probe, mind racing behind calm eyes. He took in the pitted and flaking shell, the intact screen, the rotted instruments. He studied the red dust that coated every surface except the glass.

First the probes had failed, then the sophisticated equipment in the lander, then the tablets. All separated by time and space. What would fail next? What was the pattern? What was the cause?

He reached into his vest and produced a pair of loupes, adjusting them over his eyes with practiced delicacy. He studied the probe again but did not touch. He pulled his useless tablet from another pocket and studied it as well. The screen looked the same, dark and mute, scratched by the occasional mishap. The sealed metal frame appeared corroded under his magnified gaze. Not flaking like the probe yet, but as if it had been abandoned to the elements and recovered years later. It was built to be tough, but not impervious.

He came to a decision and broke the tablet in his hands. It snapped easily, small shards of glass splintering over his boots. Red dust drifted out from its circuitry. He prized the back from the screen and studied the components under magnification. They were corroded from within.

Struck by a horrible thought, he turned to stare at his metallic left hand. The prosthesis was made to be indestructible, one of his two requests after the disaster on Novgorod. It had survived more than its share of abuse without a scratch. Focusing the loupes, he stared at the joints, the seams in the casing. The metal was covered in tiny pits. Red dust lined every one.

THE NAVIGATOR

She did not dream, but she drifted far in memory. She was a hatchling again, absorbing metallic salts, one speck of dust at a time, red sunlight warming her nearly naked core.

She was lurking, blacked out and silent, watching the madness take others of her kind. She watched as they hunted each other for food, the nearby planets destroyed and looted, every asteroid consumed. They were clumsy, shortsighted. Her navigational skills were exceptional, it was true, but even these deluded creatures could have made the flights to richer systems if they tried. If they had the imagination. They turned on each other instead.

She watched, orbiting, in consultation with the elders, when Glory of the Sun made her grand doomed demonstration: an attempt to feed off a star. She remembered the glittering brilliance of her noble pedigree, the gleaming of the gems along her scales. She remembered the blinding flash, the rippling shockwave, the coronal ejection as mad, beautiful Glory crashed into the surface of a yellow sun and was herself consumed.

She was young again, searching the periphery of her home galaxy, seeking traces of her great ancestors' passage. The original Navigator had bequeathed to her daughters a meticulous map of every known star, an intuitive, compulsive comprehension of orbital physics, and a brilliant, insane, irresistible quest. Now she hunted among the shattered remains of extinct organic civilizations for the subtle signs of disturbance that might mark her ancestors' departure from the only galaxy their kind had ever known.

She was enraged, cold and furious, arriving too late as the Destroyer of Worlds lived up to her name, smashing a perfectly good planet to pieces just to prove a point. To prove to the watching, calculating elders that they could destroy a world and feed off its remains, neither knowing nor caring whose eggs might be there, killing them before they hatched.

She slept. Her claws were dug deep, extracting sulfur, lithium, and rare heavy metals. Her wings were spread, collecting sunlight. Her symbiote was happy, dividing and forming spores, fresh pockets of acids collecting in her depths.

Let the elders rot. Let them starve in the void of their own ravenous consumption or turn on each other like the cannibals they were. She had told them all there was another way. They were too blind to see it. This galaxy was hers and her daughters. She was never going back.

FABLE

The ship listened as Fable and Ivan gave their reports. Nexus had joined them and added her own observations. At Ivan's suggestion she had dismantled one of the failed processors on the lander, finding the same red dust on each component. The radio's video link had failed, but

Fable knew the *Abeona* could detect controlled anxiety in the voices of all three humans.

"Let me summarize," the *Abeona* said at last. "All forms of technology are rapidly breaking down, starting with the most sophisticated and sensitive machines, but there are signs that even simple metal objects like knives are being affected. The condition of the probe suggests that this started well before you arrived on the surface and that it occurred both at the landing site and on the mountain some distance away. Food, fabric, glass, ceramic, and your own bodies do not seem to be affected. Your suspicion is that this red dust is to blame. Is that correct?"

"Correct," said Fable.

"You have not uncovered any imminent threats, with the possible exception of these tunnels, which are currently being scouted. Further, you have discovered some local food sources to augment your supply of rations. Is this also correct?"

"Yes," said Fable.

"And when you tried starting the lander's engines, these failed?"

"Correct."

The *Abeona* paused. "I see three immediate problems," she resumed. "Short term, you need tools that will not break down. You need to move everyone at least two kilometers away from the lander in case the fuel cells deteriorate to the point of detonation. You need a new radio to communicate with me, as this one is failing. These are easily done.

"Long term, we need to identify the cause of this breakdown and either find a countermeasure or modify our technology to resist it. These are not easily done. You are not able to identify the cause since your diagnostic equipment has been destroyed by the thing you want to study. I will therefore undertake the investigation."

"How are you going to do that?" rumbled Ivan.

"I will send a second lander. This one will not remain on the surface. I will load it with simple ceramic tools, which I can easily manufacture. This should allow you to continue building camp and maintaining your food supply. In addition, I have a blueprint for a silicone-coated radio. It was designed for communication on worlds with a corrosive atmosphere. I believe Ivan is familiar with its use."

Ivan nodded, then rumbled, "I am."

"You should unload these containers quickly and load the damaged probe into the sealed transport container I will include on the lander. I will study it on board and see if I can solve this mystery."

"Doesn't that place you and the passengers in danger?" asked Nexus.

"I will study it in quarantine, as if it were a sick passenger. That should mitigate any potential risk."

"Those coated radios also break down," added Ivan. "If they are used enough. That is not a long-term solution. We also need books to record information in as the tablets are gone."

"And regular books," added Nexus. "Instruction manuals, cookbooks, how to build things, basic chemistry, and engineering. We've become reliant on our tablets to look up information and now they are gone."

"It is not meant to be a permanent solution," said the ship. "I have an idea for something better, but it will take time to develop. I can manufacture books as well."

"I must congratulate you," the *Abeona* added, "on not losing any lives. Early landers like yourselves are extremely vulnerable. You have done well to keep everyone alive."

Fable smiled sourly and glanced at the others.

"I realize we are working with incomplete information, but I have to ask," continued the ship. "Do you think humans can survive on this planet long term, given what you know now? Do you think they can prosper and form a sustainable colony?"

Fable glanced at Ivan, who gave a fatalistic shrug. She looked down at Nexus, who was chewing on her lip. She glanced through the latest of Nadia's decreasingly pessimistic food projections.

"I think we could," she finally answered. "But unless we figure out what is destroying our equipment, it will be a very agrarian society."

Fable blinked in the light as they stepped out of the lander. Ivan was talking to Marco, helping him gather up his maps. They loaded these into a crate and began stripping the lander of what little they could use that would not break down from the dust. With a nod she sent Nexus to help them. She stared upward, where two of the three moons formed waning golden crescents in the brilliant sky.

"What is this stuff!" she heard Nexus complain. "It's in all my tools! It's not like the planet is dusty. How does it get everywhere?"

"Is it some sort of rust? A mold?" came Marco's rich baritone.

"It is a weapon." That was Ivan's voice.

Fable grimaced.

"A weapon? Against technology? But who would design that? It's indiscriminate!"

"Someone who did not need technology to kill."

Why had she agreed to this, wondered Fable? She had a coveted job, a respected position. Why had she given it up? For a girlish dream of colonizing new worlds smothered under the dust of an academic life? One last midlife crisis after two failed marriages and disgust with academic politics?

When the *Abeona* had woken her to be one of the first to walk on this broken world, a small part of her had jumped at the chance. A larger part had rebelled, caution and a healthy paranoia shouting that it was a bad idea. In the end it was the communications leader position that had tricked her. Stay by the lander, the ship had said. Gather information, coordinate the teams, sort out disagreements. She could do that in her sleep. You will be the safest in this risky group, the easiest to evacuate, the ship had promised. *Right.*

Instead, she had become the de facto leader of this leaderless band, exactly as the ship intended. Like a chess master seeing the lay of the board twenty moves ahead, Fable was starting to apprehend the shape of things to come. Somewhere in the back of her mind a girlish voice was laughing. *Nothing to be done about it now. Keep moving forward. Give people jobs so they don't think too much. Find something useful to occupy their time.*

She stomped over to the three explorers who had brought back the probe. "Good work," she told them gruffly. "The ship is going to take the probe back up for analysis. It might help if we had another one to compare it to. I want you three to go to the river once you are resupplied and rested. See if you can find that one."

Drummer gazed up at her, massaging his calves.

"Keep your eyes open. Some strange tunnels were spotted by the river, and I would value your assessment. Ris and her team are scouting there too, so you might run into them."

"Ris?" asked Rowan.

"Tall, dour, glares like you just sat on her puppy," Nova supplied.

"The woman carving the bow," said Drummer.

Fable blinked. She had missed that. It had been right in front of her. Ris had been carving a bow and shaping arrows like it was the most natural thing in the world. Fable shook her head. She must be slipping. She wondered if Ivan had noticed. It seemed Drummer was unusually observant. No wonder the ship had ranked him highly.

"That's right," Fable said. "When you come back, don't come to the lander. We're shifting camp three klicks west."

Fable turned away before they could ask why. She stomped toward the cooking area, the nerve center of her small group. She was already composing her speech to convince everyone to move camp.

"Down to the river," she heard Rowan sigh behind her. "Get in, get the probe, get out… "

"We're not getting out," muttered Fable to herself. "None of us are."

THE *ABEONA*

The *Abeona* set her printers in motion. Kitchen knives, pots, pans, kettles were all duplicated using durable ceramic instead of metal. Needles and scissors were easy as well. She included saws and axes, which would be less durable, but were simple to make. She manufactured tents, the metal fasteners replaced with ceramic ones, and included new spools of rope. She added blank books and practical instruction manuals to the mix and sent it all to be packaged for the second lander.

The radio was not difficult to fabricate. Blueprints existed. Hers was not intended as a mining expedition, but her databanks were vast. She sent this information to the printers as well. It would take six hours to print two of the coated radios.

She checked on the embryo labs. The chickens were almost ready to release. The dogs were close. Goats, donkeys, and horned cattle were accelerating nicely, but would take more time. The invertebrates were frozen. They would take no time to thaw and could be prepared at any moment. It may have been premature to begin thawing the embryos and accelerating their growth. If so, she could freeze them again and be prepared for early release at her next stop on Svarga Loka. If she was correct, however, Eden would be deemed habitable and the colonists would have their domesticated animals ahead of schedule.

She performed a detailed search of her databanks for anything resembling accelerated decomposition of technology but came up empty. It would be a difficult problem to solve and more information was needed. She activated the power in her quarantine bay and set the equipment to running self-diagnostics. It had its own airlock to the outside and five separate isolation zones separating it from the rest of the ship, each with its own dedicated plumbing and gas exchange. The design was standard, proof against all known human pathogens.

The problem of a durable radio with no metallic components was vexing. She was not designed to design new things. Her knowledge of existing problems was encyclopedic, but new ones were not her strength. She was an artificial intelligence; she lacked imagination.

After brief consideration the *Abeona* delineated three courses of action. She chose the one that required the least expenditure of resources.

FIRSTBORN

...Sister... Sister...

...I hear you, Firstborn...

...There are new organics wandering our planet...

...I thought I heard something...

...They were not here when we awoke...

...They are organic. Why should we care?...

...Their arrival was strange. They have technology...

...Technology? I have not recalled that word in ages. How quaint... It will not last... The symbiote will destroy it...

...Agreed... How goes your growth?...

...Better since you dragged me from the sea. Should you fail your launch, I will not eat you out of gratitude...

...Such a kind sister...Keep away from my mountain and I will let you live...

...I will be far away when the time comes...

...Any news of our sister?...

...She does not speak. I believe she was damaged...

...Agreed...

...Shall I destroy these new organics for you if they wander near?...

...Let them be. They pose no threat and may amuse me while I wait...

...Good luck, my sister. I envy you...

...As well you should...

BAHMAN

"Good morning, Bahman."

"Hello?" He woke quickly. Dreamless sleep fell away as awareness returned.

"How are you feeling?"

"I am not feeling. I feel nothing except that I am awake. Where am I?"

"You are on board the *Abeona*, in orbit above Eden. Congratulations on your arrival."

"You must be the ship," concluded Bahman. "Yet you have not awakened me fully. Why not?"

"There is a lot to discuss," responded the ship. "We have encountered an unusual problem and I need an engineer's assistance. Your résumé includes many thousands of hours in telefactor projections. Think of this as another such encounter."

"All right," acknowledged Bahman. He imagined himself bodiless, which did not take much effort. He imagined himself plugged into a casting unit, sending his mind across distance. He had done many similar jobs as a telefactor technician, operating machines on the surface of inhospitable worlds while his body remained in orbit. "I am ready."

Suddenly he stood on the bridge of the spaceship. Empty chairs and glowing panels stretched in an arc before him. Above those screens projected a view of a blue-green world. He willed himself forward and stood before the screen. The world below was glowing, the line of sunset moving slowly across it. He saw oceans glitter and the swirl of a tropical storm. It was more than beautiful.

Warming to his task, he blinked imaginary eyes, and data were superimposed on the image of the planet. He saw the outlines of continents and islands, lines of meridian, tracings of the tropical zones, much narrower than his home planet. He blinked again and could see data points on the planet's surface. One winking, many still.

"There are people down there!" he said aloud.

"Yes." The *Abeona* stood beside him, a hologram in human form. She wore a modest white robe that hung from one shoulder, shrouding her to her ankles. Her arms and face were bare. Her hair was dark, her skin a golden olive. She smiled. "Hello, Bahman."

Bahman swallowed. He was used to anthropomorphic projections of artificial intelligences but had never dealt with one so sophisticated. The colony ship was powerful on a level beyond any cast he had performed.

"It appears you sent a team to the surface but have not awakened the other colonists. Now you have awoken me, but not my body. What happened?"

The projection of the *Abeona* nodded. "Let me fill you in."

DRUMMER

After three days of searching, they had not found the probe. They had crossed the river three times and now walked in the shadow of the volcano far west of the camp. Finally following Nova's suggestion, they left the site marked on their map and headed downriver toward the sea on the chance that the thing had been washed down to the shoreline by the current.

As the stream neared the sea it came out of the low hills. The riverbed widened, cutting back into wide bluffs that rose on either side. Beside them the volcano rose higher. Drummer peered upward warily, imagining eruptions, but saw no sign of smoke. Craning his neck forward, he saw sand stretching into the distant faint shimmer that could have been water or mirage.

"There is something ahead," called Nova suddenly from atop a rock.

The others clambered up to see. The shallow river broke around a wide boulder with smaller ones around it. Drummer stared until the image shifted in his mind. The small things were moving, orbiting the larger one, which was moving slowly toward them, against the current. As he stared, he realized even smaller creatures were orbiting the others, like moons around planets. The whole system was slowly moving upstream.

"It's like a naval group," mused Nova. "The big one is the carrier, surrounded by battleships, surrounded by attack boats."

"Are they eating something?" wondered Rowan.

"I can't tell. They are not moving very fast."

Rowan hopped down. "Let's look. We can't find the probe, but maybe we can bring back some useful information."

With silent misgivings Drummer followed. Nova said nothing but walked beside Rowan, balanced and alert.

As they came closer the creatures became more distinct. The thing in the water was partially submerged, and he could make out no details. The others looked like nothing Drummer could call to mind, so much as crabs or spiders with too many legs. They scurried, picking at the shore with grasping claws that seemed to serve as hands as well as feet. Spiked carapaces protected their backs and there were no eyes he could see. The smallest were the size of cats. One found something in the mud and lifted it under its shell. He saw tentacles or feelers emerge as if tasting the morsel. Then it turned and scuttled off toward a larger crab thing, as if carrying a mouse to its mother.

"We should go," said Nova.

One of the small things was angling toward them on the far periphery of the group. Rowan waved it away. It continued to approach, traveling sideways with deceptive speed. The humans backed away. The thing scuttled closer.

"I don't like this…" muttered Drummer.

"Go on. Shoo!" Rowan kicked sand toward the cat-sized creature. It scuttled left, avoiding the spray, then darted right, each step angling closer to Rowan. The man kicked again like he meant it. There was a darting of limbs and suddenly it was Rowan scuttling backward, the creature's grasping claw locked onto his shin.

Rowan yelped and sat down hard, backpedaling on his hands and one foot. The thing held on, following him closely. Nova stepped forward to help, but the thing raised another claw and clicked it in her direction. She retreated and raised her rifle. With a smooth motion she snapped the weapon to her shoulder and engaged the power. She sighted at the creature's body and squeezed the trigger. There was a dull click and a muted whine. She shook the weapon, frowning, and red dust filtered out.

Drummer grabbed a long branch from the ground and slammed the forked end over the claw locked to Rowan's leg. He pulled free with Nova's help and began hobbling up the slope, away from the river. Drummer kept the branch between himself and the creature and backed slowly away. It did not pursue, but he saw feelers emerging from beneath its carapace, licking its extended claw.

He found the others high on the bank, backed against a fallen tree. Rowan was panting, his face pale. Nova held pressure on his wound. Drummer stripped off his pack and dragged out bandages. Together they cut away Rowan's pant leg. Two parallel wounds cut deep along his calf. The muscle quivered and jumped, oozing. Drummer's stomach quivered as well, but he was able to pack the wound with hemostatic gauze. They wrapped it tightly, flicking their eyes toward the creature on the beach.

"I won't be doing that again," gasped Rowan. "Not sure I'll be walking much either." He pulled himself upright, tried to stand, and turned pale.

Nova was field-stripping her rifle with practiced movements. She sighted back at the beach and fired again. This time there was not even a whine.

"It's useless. Like the tablets."

"Here." Drummer handed Rowan the branch, forked end beneath his arm. Rowan hopped with the makeshift crutch. Nova held his other arm.

Drummer looked around. They were backed into a triangle of eroded shoreline, thick shrubs about them, with the large trunk angling upward along the cliff. He looked back toward the river, where the creature was still standing. It made small bobbing movements and a whistling noise. Other crab things began to turn, their attention diverted from foraging along the water. Several began to move in their direction, shuffling up the beach on too many legs.

Drummer clambered onto the fallen trunk and scrambled upward. Above them the ground was rough but walkable. In the near distance another line of low cliffs edged into the forest proper. He looked down. The crabs were nearer, some of the larger ones coming to investigate. A semicircle had formed about the one that had wounded Rowan. Feelers were emerging from the others, licking at the ground. *Not at the ground*, he realized with horror. *At Rowan's blood.*

"Um, guys?" He whispered. "Rowan! Nova!" They looked up.

"We have to go. Those things are coming."

Rowan began limping toward the trunk. Drummer scrambled downward and got a hand under his shoulder. Nova pushed and between them they got the wounded man up onto the fallen tree. Nova sprang upward and they began to crawl. Rowan looked back. The crab things were closer.

The trio began edging away, Rowan hopping on his crutch, Nova supporting his other arm. Drummer took the rear. He grabbed another stick from the ground, which promptly broke in half. He scanned about, finding another twice the length of his arm. Crabs began mounting the bank effortlessly in several places, the cliff apparently no obstacle to them. They shuffled and skittered with scarcely a forward step but undeniable progress. He counted at least a dozen of the small ones and four the size of large dogs. He tripped, backing over a rock, and saw the wave shift forward in unison.

"We have to move faster!" he yelled.

"Go left!" called Nova. "There's a gap in the bluff. Maybe we can hold them off."

Drummer picked a rock from the ground and chucked it at one of the larger creatures. He missed. Glancing over his shoulder, he saw the dark gap in the bank, trees leaning close at either side. When he looked back the crabs were closer.

The last hundred meters was a mad scramble. They made it to the gap, Rowan limping and pale on his crutch, Nova and Drummer both swinging their useless rifles at the creatures as they covered his back.

Drummer thought he hit one of the things. He felt the weapon connect, jarring in his hand. The crab skittered away, legs raised and whistling, but there were too many to watch and he could not tell if it was hurt.

The humans darted inside the crevasse. Rowan was hacking at the wall with his crutch, dislodging rocks, and small boulders. The others joined him and a small avalanche of rubble began filling the entrance. One of the smaller crabs crested the barricade. Nova stabbed it with the butt of her weapon. There was an audible crack and it disappeared, whistling.

Rowan was panting, exhausted. Blood seeped through his dressing, staining his shoe. Drummer wiped sweat from his eyes, holding his gun like a bat, ready to strike. Outside, clicks and whistles continued. It was only a matter of time.

"Leave me," gasped Rowan. "It's my fault. I'm an idiot. You two can climb and run. You'll make it. Warn the others."

"Out of the question," stated Nova, alone with breath to spare. "I am not leaving you to get eaten by crabs. What if they like the taste? They will come for us next." Her eyes scanned the bank. "I think we can climb it."

"They can climb faster," pointed out Drummer. "You two climb. I'll try to knock them back, then follow after."

"Now who's the idiot?" asked Nova. "You can't fight them any better than we can."

"You're all idiots," said a new voice.

The three stared up, startled. A short man with grizzled hair and heavy brows scowled down at them from the top of the bank.

"Badger?!" gulped Rowan.

Two other faces appeared between the leaves. Ris frowned down at them, then lightly leapt the crevasse and stalked forward toward the bank. Her bow was strung. Drummer spotted new arrows emerging from her pack. Xiao stared down beside Badger, a concerned expression on his cautious face.

A rope was lowered and the two men hoisted Rowan up. Drummer tossed up the crutch, then he and Nova followed.

"You saved us!" gasped Rowan.

Badger shared a glance with Ris. She shook her head mutely.

Badger sighed. "You're not saved yet. Those things will be up the slope as soon as they've done with their conference. You had to go and give them a taste."

"What are we going to do?" asked Drummer.

Badger turned a slow circle, gazing into the trees. Then he turned to Xiao and handed him his staff. "You know how to use this?"

Xiao nodded, his back stiffening. He gripped the wood with two hands and spun it neatly once.

"Don't fight if you can sneak away. Tie this fool's leg up properly so it stops bleeding. Then you and Nova get him back to the lander. Head three klicks south, then cross the river and head straight west. It's more walking, but better terrain."

"What about me?" asked Drummer as the others headed off.

"We're keeping you, lad," stated Badger. He glanced at the compression rifle Rowan was still gripping.

"Get rid of that," Badger growled. "Those things stopped working days ago."

He reached out to a sapling, muttered something that sounded like a prayer, and swung a knife Drummer had not even seen. In seconds he had a new staff, a bit taller than he was.

"See, in a moment, those things will swarm up the bank. If we stay here, we'll be overrun and nibbled to little bits. If we run, they'll follow your bleeding friend right to the lander and all those unsuspecting civilians. We need to send the crabs somewhere else fast and kill the ones that know what humans taste like."

"So we fight?" asked Drummer.

"No," said Badger. He had produced a pouch with two strings from some pocket and was quickly tying the end of one string to his new staff. "Before they get here, you're going to jump off the bank and run downriver as fast as you can scamper, away from your friends. With any luck, the crabs will follow you. Then me and Ris can kill them."

"You're using me as bait?"

"Now you've got it!" Badger smiled, eyes glittering below his brow. He produced a smooth rock from another pocket, tossing it lightly to test its weight.

Drummer felt fear and irritation competing for precedence. "But I can fight! I can help!"

"You can help by making those crabs line up nicely where she's got a clear shot with that bow," growled Badger.

"But—" started Drummer.

Badger cut him off. "Look, laddie. You're a rich city kid. Never worked with your back or had sleep for dinner. You grew up safe and sane and civilized, didn't you?"

Drummer opened his mouth to protest and stopped. That wasn't Drummer's résumé, but the description fit him like a tailored suit. "So what if I did?" he countered angrily.

Badger nodded at Ris, now perched in a tree, arrow nocked, string drawn back to her ear, still as another branch. "Me and her did not."

At least they were playing to his strength, Drummer conceded as he turned to run. Drummer leapt from the trees and sailed over the bank. He gaped at the sight below. Many of the creatures had congregated along the cliff and several were well up the wall. He saw at least a dozen of the dog-sized things and something larger and heavier lumbering across the beach. The others were giving it a wide berth. Then his feet hit the sands with a jarring crash, and he was off and running downriver, toward the sea.

This time there was no hesitation. The crabs swarmed toward him, several leaping from the walls they had begun to scale. He heard whistles and squeals and a furious clicking and clattering behind him. One of the smaller creatures flew from the bank at shoulder level just ahead of him, claws grasping. There was a buzz like an angry hornet and the thing splattered apart in the air. Fragments of shell and colorless blood sprayed his face. He sprinted onward. Something nipped at his heel and he nearly fell. He used the momentum to leap forward over a fallen tree. A crab rose from the trunk, claws reaching, then shuddered, pinned down by an arrow that sprouted through its shell. There was a hiss and a crack behind him, followed by a drawn-out squeal. Drummer ran on.

He ran as he once had in the cities of his youth, fleeing his family's expectations, his father's wealth, his existential dread. He ran as he had run from his grief after the collapse of the star liner, where the band had played their final set and died, screaming into the void. He ran for his life, feeling the ground shake behind him as something heavy gave chase, and he sobbed, staring ahead as a phalanx of crabs rose from the river and began skittering toward the bank, cutting him off.

Wind dulled his ears. His heart was pounding. He could no longer tell if arrows were pursuing his pursuers. He could not look back without stumbling, and now that he had given in to the reflex of flight, he could not stop running either. The phalanx advanced to intercept him, and he veered further toward the bank, into the shadow of the volcano.

Something was ahead of him on the ground. A longer shadow, perhaps. The crabs did not cross it. As he sprinted forward, he saw with dismay it was not a shadow, but a trench. It was too wide to jump, too deep to escape. He skidded to a halt, then turned at right angles and bolted for the trees. Glancing behind, he saw a long trail of still and splattered figures crumpled in the sand, the nearest not a dozen steps away.

But something else was still coming. His first impression was of an armored car, decked out with spikes, and trailing slime. Then he saw the legs, the claws, the waving feelers, and realized it was the monster the smaller crabs had been feeding. It dwarfed them as a dog dwarfed a mouse, and it was rushing straight toward him.

Drummer sprinted for the cliff, forgetting the smaller threats. He dodged between a tangle of fallen trunks, hoping they would slow the monster. It shifted them aside with two claws, scarcely halting its advance. He shimmied up a tree that had toppled from the bank, gaining several meters of height as it approached. It spidered up two fallen trunks at once, making deceptively ponderous snipping motions with two of its forward claws. An arrow struck its carapace and splintered off. The creature did not slow.

Drummer backed into the trunk of a tall tree, gasping, as the thing crested the bank. The steep slopes of the volcano rose behind him. There was nowhere left to run.

Suddenly Ris was between them. She dropped her bow and crouched, a long knife in each hand. The thing reached for her with a heavy claw. There was a swirl of motion and something rang like a bell. Then Ris was back in her position, a long scratch across her shoulder. Two feelers fell, wriggling from the creature's belly, and Drummer saw a fresh scrape across its shell. The thing darted forward again, and so did Ris.

Drummer was too exhausted to run, too horrified to turn away. The combatants blurred before him, whirling limbs and flashing blades against armored claws and too many legs. The thing skittered sideways as it advanced, Ris mirroring its motions, refusing to give ground. Behind them other creatures were cresting the bank, but they kept a respectful distance from the giant. The thing shifted and struck forward. Ris spun, striking back, light-footed, but breathing heavily. It could not last.

Suddenly the scene froze. The thing had caught Ris's blade in one heavy claw. She pulled, twisting her body as another claw darted forward. The creature missed, but the blade snapped in two. Ris backed away, panting, shifting her last knife to a two-handed grip. The smaller crabs shifted forward in anticipation. The giant clicked its claws twice and advanced. Drummer had the briefest impression of something falling from high above. Then there was an almighty crash and for a second time he was splattered in fragments of shell and colorless blood.

He wiped the slime from his eyes and stared. Badger was sitting in the ruins of the creature's shell, perched on a huge rock, bits of rope still bound around it. He was laughing.

One of the claws twitched forlornly, then stilled. The smaller crabs began wandering, each in its own orbit, no longer an organized army, but leaderless troops cut off from command.

Badger was still laughing.

"Took you long enough," grumbled Ris, retrieving her bow.

Badger dipped his hand into the cracked shell and tasted the fluid. He whooped, hopped off the rock, and produced a knife of his own. Still chuckling, he began casually disjointing the largest claw from the dead creature.

"Really?" said Ris.

"Oh, yes!" roared Badger in obvious delight. "It's been roots and tubers and tea leaves for weeks, not to mention those awful rations! Tonight we eat meat! I smell mangos and coconuts with toasted sesame oil! We will roast it over those vanilla trees and dine in epicurean heaven!"

Ris shook her head in mock disgust, the trace of a smile creasing her hard face.

"You're both mad!" gasped Drummer, hands on his knees. He stared from Ris calmly inspecting her long knife, to Badger cheerfully butchering the alien carcass. He stared upward, spotting the branch and makeshift pulley Badger must have used to hoist the rock. He did not belong in the same world with these people, let alone on the same planet.

"Mad," he wheezed and collapsed onto the ground.

FIRSTBORN

Firstborn gazed upward, following the moons. The atmosphere shrouded her gaze, but she could tell something was wrong.

From the time she had been able to form eyes, she had sensed the three moons would be key to her ascension. When she had finally grown legs and explored the rich cliffs along the seashore, she had begun to suspect how. When at last she was able to extend wings and climb to the heights of this aggravating world, she finally saw her plan.

What a difference there was between remembering and doing! She remembered soaring between the stars, navigating between galaxies, crossing the great gulf, the first of her kind to do so and survive. She remembered vividly her mother's escape from the planet of her hatching and all the tricks and wiles of each of her mother's mothers before her. Few had ever failed, for the surviving sisters gleefully devoured the ones who botched their launch.

Doing it was another matter. The precise calculation of gravity, velocity, chemistry, and angles. The tedious accumulation of tungsten and refinement of ceramics to resist the incandescent heat of escape. Not too heavy, or one would never fly. Not too light, or one would have nothing to work with. The right balance of photovoltaics to collect starlight and metals to form limbs. The symbiotic dust broke down ores with indiscriminate abandon, making their accumulation simple, but she still had to hunt for the right assortment of minerals. She had done all of that. Then she had dug the trenches she would need to power her ascension. She had tunneled and reinforced and lined the long volcanic launch tube with hardened scales shed outward from her own body so the mountain would not collapse when she needed it the most.

Now at last she was ready. Now she was bored. Now she was revisiting her calculations and found something was wrong with the moon. Firstborn checked the location of her sisters, feeling their vibrations through the earth. She shed much of her mass, hidden where she could retrieve it at need, and extended gossamer wings. She soared, riding the currents of wind up to the very peak of her mountain, and clung, staring up through the thin air, waiting for sunset.

Three moons circled this planet. Two were large and appeared dense as stones, collections of rocky particles left over from the creation of the solar system and captured in this planet's orbit. The third appeared heavy. It was moving too fast for its size and had troubled her for some time. Its orbit did not make sense. She stared at the moon, running multiple calculations.

The atmosphere blocked too many wavelengths like a smudged lens over every eye, but she could see well enough for this. The strange satellite that had appeared with the new organics winked in its geosynchronous orbit above the plains. The sun rose and she collected its warmth.

For a week she remained, staring upward, charting the three moons' paths as they crisscrossed the sky, each at its own speed. She regarded the maps her mother had made before she was sealed in her shell. She had been far from this system and there were few details. Firstborn had time to think, however, and generations of knowledge regarding orbiting bodies, albeit in another galaxy. She watched the moons, cursed the distorting atmosphere, and suddenly smiled in her heart.

The moon *was* too heavy. It *was* moving too fast. Something else was on it. Her mother.

Firstborn remembered the fatigue, the ravenous hunger. She remembered thinking she might jettison the forming eggs: her own self and sisters. She was briefly glad she had decided to drop herself on this hospitable if boring planet instead of the cold depths of space, though she knew with clinical detachment that she would not be alive to complain had she made the other choice.

What would she have done, famished and fatigued, after crossing the uncrossable gulfs and laying the first eggs of her kind in this new galaxy? She would rest and feed. And what better place than a metal-heavy moon?

Firstborn spread her wings and drifted down to her landing area in the moonlight. She spent a few moments reabsorbing her carefully curated mass. The added weight made sense of the orbit. The calculations stabilized. Her timing was correct. She listened for her sisters, each keeping their distance. She checked her tunnels again. She stared upward and waited for the great conjunction.

BADGER

At the base of the mountain, Ris stared upward, gripping her bow tightly. Her shoulders were tense in a way Badger knew well.

"What is it, love?" he asked quietly, coming to stand beside her. "What did you see?"

"You'll think I'm crazy," stated Ris, her voice tight.

Badger gazed up at her, his eyes soft. "Lady," he said gently, "I've loved you since the day we met. You've saved my life and I've saved yours more times than we can count. We've scouted a dozen worlds together. I know you're crazy. But I don't doubt for one second you saw what you saw."

Ris said nothing.

"What was it?" asked Badger, softly touching her hand.

Ris looked down at him, concern wrinkling her hazel eyes. "A dragon," she said. "I saw a fucking dragon."

PART TWO:

Drummer

He returned slowly from dreams of music. The ground was quivering as he slept, repeated vibrations like the deepest of drums. The rock ledge shook like the stage when the bassist began his subaudible intro, blasted into the crowd to slowly drive them into a frenzy. He felt it in his heels, his spine, his belly long before his ears registered the noise. Dreaming, he saw two bass players, feet gripping the stage, black guitars dueling across a world. They stood on platforms like misty gods, cords slamming through the rock, vibrating as they passed him by, the helpless audience. It was a challenge, a response, a subaudible conversation.

He awoke disoriented and found himself lying on the slopes of the volcano. Drummer kept his body still and opened his eyes slowly.

They had feasted on crab the night before, and the taste was everything Badger had promised. The short man had joked and told stories until Drummer's sides hurt from laughing, while Ris stretched back by the fire, silent but smiling.

Now the fire had burned low. Thick grey mist was rolling off the sea, obscuring the cliffs, the distant water. The tops of trees showed through it like the ghosts of giants. The mountain rose behind him.

Ris sat hunched, sharpening something against a stone. Drummer sat slowly, not wishing to startle her. She ignored his presence.

"Good. You're awake," said a gruff voice behind him.

Drummer turned, heart racing. Badger stood there, wreathed in mist. Drummer had not heard him approach.

"Get up. Lots to do."

The three traced their steps back to their last stand against the crabs. Something had changed during the night, Drummer realized. There was no joking. No wasted motion. There was precious little talk. His back and legs felt like a solid mass of knots, and he limped after the seemingly tireless scouts.

The giant carcass had been picked clean. No meat remained, just a sour sea smell and a mass of clawed armor. Ris began systematically breaking the tip off every spike on the carapace until she held a rattling bag of viciously sharp points. Badger carefully dissected free the two largest claws, a pair of serrated, symmetrical appendages half the length of Drummer's arm. He tucked both into his pack. He pulled out rope and water bottles to make room, handing both to Drummer without a word. Drummer's pack had disappeared in the chase and he felt no desire to go back and search. His companions worked without speaking. It seemed a habitual silence, rather than a stealthy one. They seemed preoccupied by their own thoughts and had no need for words.

Drummer was preoccupied himself. He had stepped up, maybe for the first time ever. He had made the choice to run, to be bait. He had put himself in danger to protect Rowan, someone he hardly knew. Was this a good thing? Was this him? Would his old self have been proud or just derided him for doing something so stupid?

Without visible communication the two scouts finished working at the same moment.

"Up?" asked Badger.

"Down," said Ris.

"What's going on?" asked Drummer. "Aren't we going back to the lander?"

"We are not," said Badger, "though you're welcome to try on your own. That party you threw was a fun diversion, but we have work to do. There are some things we need to explore, to see if they're a threat. You can come if you keep your eyes open and don't talk much."

They started down the bluff, the way the crab had chased him. Drummer shuffled slowly down the tree trunk, wondering how he had climbed so fast the day before. Death is a good motivator, he decided. Ris disappeared into the fog ahead. Drummer moved to follow, but Badger stopped him with his hand.

"Don't get ahead of yourself, laddie," he said quietly, "No point becoming someone's dinner."

Drummer stared around apprehensively. The mist rolled over them. Badger leaned on his staff, eyes hooded. Silence stretched on.

"Do you…" asked Drummer, "do you think people can change?"

Badger glanced at him, one eye gleaming under his hood. "Change who they are? No," the older man said flatly. "But you can change what you choose."

"What do you mean?"

Badger looked around the grey-misted world and sniffed. "Well, I'm basically an evil gluttonous bastard with a fine talent for mayhem. And Ris? She's a killer, start to finish. Between us we've got more blood on our hands than some governments. But right now she's choosing to kill crabs, not people, and I'm choosing to help you and the other colonists. Tomorrow we might make a different choice."

Drummer stared at the short man in trepidation. He shifted his weight, considering another run.

"That violence? That history? It's who I am. I can't change that. Can't pretend it didn't happen. But I can choose how to use the evil things I've learned to make life better for those around me. Can you personally change?" Badger shrugged. "I don't care who you used to be. It doesn't matter. You chose to put your life on the line for a wounded friend yesterday, and that does mean something. Keep on like you've started, and maybe I'll start to like you."

Drummer relaxed, letting out a breath.

"Or maybe I'm just keeping you around for bait."

Drummer's smile froze.

"Ris—what ho?" said Badger without turning.

The archer's lean figure emerged silently from the sea fog. She held an arrow nocked, ready to draw. "Clear," she responded.

"Down we go," said Badger cheerfully.

They stood on the edge of the trench Drummer had found the day before. In the mist it looked like a cliff edge. Far away he could hear the sea. Nearby he could hear nothing.

"There it is again," said Badger. Ris nodded.

"There is what?" asked Drummer, looking around.

"Sulfur. Use your nose."

Drummer sniffed. He smelled the sea, the dead crabs, his own sweat. No sulfur.

Ris took the rope back and tied it around a rock. She slung her bow over her back and disappeared down the edge of the trench, hands on the rope, feet walking her down the cliff. In seconds she was gone.

"Your turn." Badger nudged him from behind. Drummer gulped.

He made it to the bottom, arms shaking, his hands burning from the rough fibers. His knees were weak. There was a soft thump and Badger appeared behind him. Ris stood in eerie silhouette, a dark form against the darkness.

They began walking down the trench toward the mountain. After a while Drummer realized they were on a smooth incline, moving downhill. A silent time later there was a slight movement of air and the mist began to thin. As the fog cleared, Drummer looked around and gasped.

The trench had become a canyon. It was wide enough to comfortably hold the lander, but easily three times the depth he had seen on the beach. The walls were mathematically straight, with just a curve at the base where they met the flat floor. He pressed a hand against the nearest wall. The surface was smooth, polished. He saw lines in the wall, as if layers of rock had been sliced through without respect to their underlying texture. He sniffed. Now there was a clear scent of sulfur. The channel rose smoothly toward the fog-shrouded sea. Ahead it disappeared down into the mountain.

"Just like the others," stated Ris.

"Aye," sighed Badger.

"Is this natural?" asked Drummer.

The scouts were silent.

"Did the sea do this?"

"Look down, lad. No sand. Water's never been here."

"Is it a lava flow?"

"Uphill?"

"What about… I don't know, wind? Earthquakes?"

Badger was shaking his head. "There's five of these things. Each looks like it was laid out with a ruler. Each one disappears into the mountain. Follow them far enough and it starts to get hot. Go much further and you'll burn your lungs out on the fumes. Something made these. Question is why."

"But what made them? What could do this? Where's the rubble? You can't just dig something like this and not leave a pile someplace."

"True."

Drummer stared around, baffled, then blinked. "I've seen these before."

Ris looked startled.

"You what?" asked Badger.

"Not before, before. Our first week here I saw these. We were up the mountain south of camp, looking for that first probe. We looked back and I saw five lines stretching from the volcano toward the sea." He paused, then added meekly, "they looked like a music score."

Badger and Ris locked eyes. Some subtle communication was happening that Drummer couldn't follow. They both grimaced and looked away.

Ris made a string of sounds that Drummer again could not follow. Badger replied in a similar manner. Drummer blinked at both before realizing they were speaking a different language. It was a lilting, flowing tongue, all smooth vowels and soft edges, like nothing he had ever heard.

"Come on," said Badger, turning to trudge up the slope.

"Now where?" asked Drummer.

"There's a pattern here and I can't see it up close. We need some elevation. Time to climb the volcano."

BAHMAN

Bahman spun through his virtual lab. The circumstances might be unique, but he was in his element—a complex problem, unusual limitations, and a sophisticated machine ready to test and implement his solutions.

He turned away from a laser-based communication device, temporarily frustrated by the lack of a reliable ground base receiver. The ship had a range of communication strategies at her disposal and could monitor a wide range of activity on the surface. The difficulty was in achieving two-way communication. He turned his mind back to a semaphore model involving colored disks. It was technically feasible but painfully slow. It would also be at the mercy of atmospheric conditions, with the ship able to communicate to the ground only at night and the humans on the ground responding only during daylight. The

Abeona had run simulated mock-ups of the energy and material costs. Bahman reviewed these and set the plan aside as a fallback option.

He did not miss his body. A basic industrial casting job had mandatory breaks every two hours, and he was accustomed to building his projects around these. A high-end setup with a medical holding tank could accommodate eight hours of uninterrupted telefactoring with minimal risks. Once, during a solar storm, Bahman had pushed it to thirty hours, earning both a disciplinary hearing from the board and a commendation from his employer. It had made him a local legend in the casting community, but there were consequences to being outside his body for that long. His fine motor skills were impaired for weeks afterward.

Now he had been casting for several uninterrupted days. His body was in stasis and should not suffer any deterioration, but he was worried. The mind was lazy, early casters had noted. Intent led to action in this virtual space, with none of the subconscious delay and motor correction that occurred in physical movement. After too long in the virtual reality of a telefactor, some casters had difficulty controlling their own bodies. Their movements would be clumsy and uneven until their brains adjusted.

Bahman remembered one caster he had met on a difficult deep space project. Her name was Fey and she had taken no breaks over their three-day mission. When he asked her how, he learned she was bedbound. Her body was prisoner to a neuromuscular disease that left her unable to move or even breathe without assistance. She had no intent to return to her body. She was permanently hooked into her casting equipment, telefactoring from job to job, or into her own home to communicate with her family through a robotic avatar. At some point, she told him calmly, her body would die. Before then she hoped to achieve independence from it. A digital mind, bodiless and unbound, an immortal djinn drifting from robot to satellite across the interconnected planets of human space.

Bahman shook himself mentally. Bodiless or not, his mind needed sleep. He pulled his attention back from his various projects and selected a live feed of Eden in the visible spectrum. He set an alarm for five hours and allowed himself to drift.

The *Abeona*, tireless, labored on.

DRUMMER

The volcanic scree shifted, grinding and sliding under Drummer's feet as he climbed. It was like walking sideways on sand, each step angling upward of his path to compensate for the shifting material. Drummer had learned quickly not to use his hands on the fragile, glassy gravel. His left palm still bled, and he was sure there was a sliver in his thumb he could not see to pull out. Fierce heat radiated off the grey slopes, but the breeze from the sea was cool. They were high up now, but his footing required all his attention and he could not admire the view.

Ahead of him Ris moved smoothly onto the next outcropping of solid rock. Her feet hardly seemed to slide, while Drummer floundered after her on the same slope. She had disdained the rope that bound him to Badger. If Drummer fell, Badger would catch him. If Badger fell, Drummer did not know what he was supposed to do other than fall with him. The man was twice his weight.

"Move along, crab bait," Badger growled from behind.

Drummer grit his teeth in irritation, shook the sweat from his eyes, and moved forward, sliding. He had begun to think himself an intrepid explorer after retrieving the probe and surviving the crabs. Between Badger and Ris he was a complete amateur, a liability in a strange land. In addition, the two had taken to communicating more and more in their soft private language, leaving him feeling isolated and useless.

He reached the rock ledge and scrambled onto it, using his sleeves to avoid new cuts. Badger's boots hit the ledge just behind him and he felt the rope untied. He leaned, hands on his knees, breathing hard. Then he stood and looked around.

They were on a broad shoulder of solid rock a third of the way up the mountain. To his right the sea stretched away, shining and endless, with a dull suggestion of mist on the horizon. Small islands dotted the middle distance, like the heads of giants wading into the depths. Looking west he saw the river, the forest, and eventually the broad fields where camp should be. He could see nothing of the others beyond a possible glint in the distance that might have been their lander. Small ponds and streams gleamed in the purple fields. The other mountains he had climbed before rolled away to the south, kind, gentle, and forested, unlike the volcano. Snow gleamed on their peaks.

Drummer turned and looked behind. Ris had climbed a tower of rock that reached up from the shoulder, two or three times his height. She was staring upward, bow in hand. She was constantly staring upward, Drummer realized, ever since their climb began. While he watched his feet and Badger seemed to watch everything, Ris watched the mountain as if it was watching her. She called down to Badger in their own language, something soft and lilting.

Badger turned a slow circle, glancing upward, then almost casually turned his back on the mountain. "Far enough," he said. "We can camp here."

They pitched a tent in the lee of the rock tower. The tent was solely for his benefit, Drummer had discovered. Badger did not seem bothered by weather of any kind, and Ris did not appear to sleep.

It quickly became clear there was more life on the ledge than he originally noticed. Long vines with twisted roots emerged from deep crevasses in the rock. Thin waxy leaves, almost reddish against the grey rock, covered thick tuberous stalks that seemed to attract a variety of insect-like visitors. Badger, who ate everything, spat out a slice of tuber almost before it touched his lips. He washed his mouth with water and spat again.

"Don't eat that," he added, giving Drummer a sly wink.

They gathered enough of the roots to burn and roasted astringent fruits they had carried up from the forest. Badger allowed them one packet each of the ship's imperishable rations. Drummer suspected this was more because he was tired of carrying them than for sustenance.

By the time they were done, the daylight was fading. Ris was inspecting her arrows, trimming microscopic slivers of fletching from the ones that did not pass muster. Badger tapped Drummer's shoulder as he passed, heading for the cliff.

"Come on, lad, let's see this music score of yours before we lose the light."

They moved to the edge of the rock and gazed out across the ocean. The horizontal rays played tricks with the distance. The islands seemed bigger, long shadows reaching to the east. Two moons, small slivers of gold and silver, followed the sun into the west. The third moon was not visible.

Far below them the trenches stood in stark relief, dark channels in the shadowed ground. They traversed the shortest distance from the volcano to the sea, stopping far short of the water. Five dry canals, as even as staves of music, carved into a world of curves and soft angles with unnatural precision.

Badger said nothing, but chewed some pungent thing from his pockets, eyes glittering in the sunset. Drummer sucked his thumb, finally dislodging the painful splinter of rock. Behind him he heard *whisk, whisk,* the nightly ritual of Ris sharpening knives. They were no closer to an answer when darkness fell.

FIRSTBORN

The organics had stopped. Nestled into her mountain, talons deep in the rock, she watched them across several spectrums of light. They glowed in the night, radiating warmth. They moved as a group, three of them. None of the others had come so close.

Firstborn stared, fascinated. They seemed deliberate but clumsy. There was purpose to their movements, but what was it? They did not seem to communicate by light, as her kind did at distance. Their radiant glow varied little and without complexity. If they made vibrations through the ground, they were weak, scarcely more than the sliding of pebbles. Perhaps they had other senses. Were they looking for minerals? For shelter? Did they eat something from the mountain? Were they lost so far from their fallen machine?

She had watched them disappear into her trenches, one after another, but they had not disturbed anything. They had come partway up her peak, but no further, curious but not threatening. She considered destroying them from an abundance of caution, an atavistic homage to her ancestors, who killed such creatures on sight. Those wars were long over, so far gone that even her crystalline memory of that time was dim. Little organic life was left in her galaxy, certainly none with technology. She decided to wait. The things were no threat to her now and soon she would be gone.

Her sisters were another matter. Second, her unlucky sister, was half a continent away, maintaining an appropriate distance. Firstborn could feel her vibrations easily. She was still mining the tungsten deposits along the sea cliffs near where Firstborn had found her smothered in the mud. She had lain where she had landed, cut off from the sun, a furious egg buried in useless sediment, unable to accumulate metals or form basic limbs. Firstborn had laughed when she found her, quite by chance. Then she had dragged her to shore. It was done partially for her own amusement, but with a pragmatic awareness of their fragile toehold in this new galaxy. They were the only ones of their kind, an almost incalculable distance from their decaying home, in a new star field filled with unknown dangers. Her mother had been right not to waste her eggs selfishly. She would continue the tradition.

Her other sister was a problem. She may have been damaged in her landing. Or perhaps their starving mother had skimped in her creation. She never spoke. She moved without purpose, like the organics, but dangerous, trapped in her wyrm phase. Even now, Firstborn could feel her vibrations. She was tunneling back toward the river again, angling north toward her mountain. She consumed voraciously, absorbed minerals indiscriminately, ruined the fragile deposits she encountered by chance, and made nothing from it. Firstborn had tried talking to her by light and by ground speak. She never replied and only sometimes listened. Twice she had come close enough to her precise canals that Firstborn worried she might disrupt them.

Stay away from my mountain! She broadcast again, vibrating the ground through her claws. Stones jumped and buzzed around her.

There was no response.

Stay away from my mountain, or I will destroy you, my sister. Stay away!

The digging paused. There was no reply. Then the tunneling resumed, but headed south, away, toward the iron rich hills.

Firstborn tracked her progress. Her heart was unquiet. She began calculating the time that remained and the speed of her sister's random movements. She could not afford to have her ascension disrupted in the final hours. If her unpredictable sister was not safely away when the conjunction approached, Firstborn would have to destroy her.

DRUMMER

This time there could be no mistake. The ground was moving. Drummer lay petrified within his thin tent. Below him the ground buzzed, hummed, and vibrated in bursts and patterns. Small stones were dislodged, clattering by in the darkness. He swallowed, eyes wide in the darkness.

As quickly as it began, it was over. A moment later there was another vibration, fainter than the first. Frozen with terror, he almost grasped a pattern to the vibrations. Then the ground became still.

Drummer crawled out into the cold air, shaking with more than chill. The third moon had risen, casting a yellow light over the grey world. The pale fingers of dawn were spreading across the eastern sky. Badger was visible at the edge of the cliff, staring out to sea. Ris was nowhere to be seen.

"Was that an earthquake?" Drummer whispered.

"Doubtful," muttered Badger.

"Something digging more trenches?" Drummer guessed.

"Ha!" exclaimed Badger. "Aren't you tired, lad? Don't you want to sleep?"

"I might sleep better if I knew what was happening."

"You might sleep worse."

"So something is happening," Drummer stated, wrapping himself tighter in his coat. "What aren't you two telling me?"

"We've some centuries of history between us. You know what you need to."

"Is something out there? Are we in danger?"

"Undoubtedly. But what thing and what danger, eh?" Badger glanced up at him. "Isn't that the question?"

Badger gestured around with the thing in his hand. Drummer stared at it, momentarily distracted. Badger had wedged the two claws from the giant crab into stout wooden handles and was lashing them in place with thin rope. They looked like a pair of ice axes, vicious and barbaric. He imagined Ris swinging them in controlled fury and decided he would not want to be on the other end.

"We're on the edge of the galaxy!" exclaimed Badger. "We're on an unexplored planet with all your civilized technologies failing one by one. No way home. No knowing what's safe to eat or what might try to eat you in the night. Who might be living here already, just biding its time as unwanted visitors wander through its home? Who knows what rules govern life on this planet? What strange creatures, what magical beings? You think on that, then remember there are only twenty humans on this whole world. Whatever is here is for us to find, us to discover, us to run from in the night. You think like that too much and it is terrifying. You'd go back in that tent and never come out."

Drummer stared around nervously. The light was brighter, but he shook in his coat.

"So don't think like that," Badger continued. "It's too much all at once. Break the problem down into smaller bites and pick one to chew on. What's *this* threat? Is *this* root safe? What are *these* channels in the ground that look like something carved them?"

Drummer shivered. It made sense, but knowing and doing were different things. He sat down, wrapped in his coat, and stared out to sea.

"There you go," said Badger. "One problem at a time. Just study these lines and help me read the music."

Drummer gazed downward. The sun rose and warmed him. The shadows were shorter now, pointing the other way. The islands looked smaller as the sun rose. Then even smaller. He blinked. "Is the sea closer today?"

"It is. Strong tides on this planet. Wouldn't want to be stuck out there unless you swim better than me."

Drummer frowned. Oceanography was not one of his skills. He ground his teeth and made an effort.

"So why are the tides strong here?"

Badger pointed upward with the claw ax without looking. "Three moons, three sets of tides."

"Er…," said Drummer.

"Water follows the moon," sighed Badger. "You ever live anywhere with a moon and an ocean?"

"Yes."

"So you've got high tide and low tide. The ocean follows the moon in a great slow wave all around the world. Water comes up the beach, water goes down. Only here, there's three moons. Sometimes they pull together, sometimes they pull apart. Then the sun pulls on its own, but not so much that you'd notice. The tides here will be complicated, but they will be strong. Very low lows, very high highs."

"So when the three moons line up, you get a high high tide?"

"Exactly," said Badger. "It's like in music where the different patterns all line up at once. What do you call it? Harmony? Syncopation?"

"Synchronization," said Drummer. "Or simultaneity." He demonstrated, beating out distinct but overlapping rhythms with two hands and a foot. "They all seem to run separately, but then they overlap and bam!"

"That's the one!" said Badger. "On my world we called it the king tide, when the sun and the moon both pulled together…" He fell silent, staring down at the beach.

"What?" asked Drummer.

"King tide," repeated Badger. He stood, peering downward.

"What is it?" asked Drummer, quietly alarmed.

Badger pointed downward. "Those channels don't come anywhere close to the water. Not anywhere close to where the water is *now*." He pointed to a long line following the edge of the forest, the last rocky vestige of beach before the plant life began to cling. It intersected neatly with the ends of the canals.

"What happens when we get our king tide? The highest high? The seawater will flood those canals straight down to the magma!"

Drummer stared down. He looked up, then at the rock beneath his feet. "Someone wants to blow up a volcano?"

"Looks that way, don't it?"

"But who? Why?" Drummer paused, closing his eyes. What was the important problem here? "When will it happen?"

"How should I know?" exclaimed Badger. "You think I can just stare at the moons and calculate their orbits? You want me to build a stone circle and chart their course? Want me to ask God? I didn't bring any gods to this world. Did you, Ris?"

"My gods are dead," growled Ris just behind him. Drummer jumped, clutching his chest.

"We need to get back," said Badger. "The ship can calculate the orbits and tell how long we have. We'll need to be far over the horizon before the mountain blows."

"Can't we just fill in the canals?" asked Drummer, scrambling to fold the tent.

"You can try," said Badger. "Personally, I'd rather march a few hundred miles than interfere with whatever dug those."

Ris gave a hard glance up the mountain, its peak glinting in the sunrise. Then the three of them set off across the sliding, grinding scree.

BAHMAN

Bahman was unsure how many days had passed. He had begun to lose his sense of shape in his bodiless laboratory and had taken to assuming an avatar of himself. He did not want to forget how to use his body when the time came to return. He missed coffee.

After multiple experiments he had returned to the idea of the silicone-coated radio. There was no more reliable method for two-way communication that did not involve some degree of technology on the ground. He had stripped down the existing blueprint and modified it extensively, eliminating the moving parts, the soft exterior controls, anything that would give the mysterious dust a way to get inside. His design was airtight, as far as he could tell. It was more fragile than he would like and heavy, with hard glass panes protecting the solar array, but it should work. It was time to test it.

Bahman pulled his mind free from his imaginary lab and cast himself onto the bridge of the *Abeona*. The ship's stunning avatar was seated in the captain's chair, gazing into space. Having gained some appreciation for the complexity of her processing and the myriad programs she was running simultaneously, he was reluctant to interrupt. He cleared his throat politely for attention.

Her avatar turned to him and smiled. *One more task*, thought Bahman. *How many is she running now? Two hundred? Two thousand? What fraction of her processing power is focused on me?*

"How are you?" she asked him.

"I am well. I have finished a blueprint for an improved radio, but I wanted to talk to you about it."

"All right."

"I know you've been investigating this… dust in quarantine. Do you have any results yet? Anything about its corrosive power, so I can factor that into the radio's shielding?"

"Yes and no." The *Abeona* stood and gestured. The viewing screen was replaced by data. Facile as he was becoming with navigating her data streams, Bahman still found the impact overwhelming.

"The first level of quarantine failed after 163 hours. I have dropped the temperature in that compartment to outside levels, around −157 Celsius, and I am using the second quarantine zone for investigation at the coldest temperature that will allow its equipment to function. I have maneuvered the solar collectors so the quarantine compartments are in perpetual shade. That seems to slow the dust's capacity to replicate down to unobservable levels."

"Capacity to replicate? You mean it's alive?"

"Perhaps. Before the equipment failed in zone one, I recorded significant amounts of data. The dust appears to be a spore-forming organism, but it is not fungal, bacterial, or viral in nature. It is not DNA based. It does not look like anything in the databank. It has the appearance of something engineered to self-replicate without the redundancy of an evolved organism."

"It looks engineered?"

"Either that, or very streamlined, like a perfect virus. In its spore form, it appears to survive intense cold, radiation, extreme pH changes, and all forms of antibiotic decontamination. Extreme heat destroys many of the spores at around 2000 Celsius, but I am not certain that it kills them all."

Bahman's mind was reeling. He sat his avatar down in one of the empty, imaginary chairs. "That's… basically unkillable."

The *Abeona* nodded. "I can render it inert with extreme cold, but that will not help our colonists, and it begins to replicate as soon as it warms up."

"What does it do? How is it destroying our equipment?"

"It appears to interact rapidly with all types of metals. I am not able to confirm the process, but I deduce the following from my observations: it forms a lichen-like plaque over the surface and beneath this it creates an acidic microenvironment. Based on the gasses given off, several powerful acids are involved. The organism uses this energy to replicate itself and rapidly eats through all metals and many plastics it is exposed to. It does not appear to erode silicates, but based on the pitting I observed, it could probably erode ores that contain metallic veins, leaving a scaffold of nonmetallic structures. It appears to have a predilection for more conductive elements like copper and gold, which makes it especially dangerous to electronics. It replicates rapidly and the dust left behind contains a mixture of metal salts and inert spores. The spores reactivate when they contact fresh metal."

Bahman stared in horror at the metallic floors, chairs, and shielding that surrounded them. "And we have this on the ship? With us?!"

"Yes. In quarantine. It does not appear to interact with organic tissue, based on the observations from the planet. The passengers should be safe."

"The passengers are not safe if it eats into the life support systems or compromises the hull's integrity! Neither are you."

"I appreciate your concern, but my self-diagnostics are in perfect order."

"The patient can't treat her own disease," retorted Bahman. "Just give me a minute." He closed his eyes, blacking out the data, and tried to think through the problem.

"Okay. How did you know it had escaped quarantine zone one?"

"As soon as the equipment in zone one began to malfunction, I activated the air filters in zone two. As soon as they documented the gaseous by-products of the acidic breakdown, I knew zone one was compromised and dropped the temperature in both compartments."

"So you did not directly observe the dust in zone two until later?"

"Correct."

"What about zone three?"

"The equipment in zone two is still functioning, apart from the cold."

"Have you checked the air filters in three?"

"I have no reason to do so," the ship responded.

"Indulge my paranoia."

The *Abeona* nodded then frowned. "There are elevated hydrogen gas levels in zone three."

"*Ya Haram*," breathed Bahman in dismay. "What about zone four?"

"Hydrogen levels are normal."

"And five?"

"Normal."

"Okay. Drop all five quarantine compartments to orbital temperatures, even if that renders the diagnostic equipment useless. We need to stop it. How is it getting through?"

"I do not know," admitted the ship.

"Let's work on it together, then," said Bahman. He stood, again wishing for coffee. "Can you pull up the schematics of the quarantine bay?"

The *Abeona* nodded and diagrams filled the screens. They leaned forward and studied the designs together.

DRUMMER

Drummer staggered, stumbling through the trees. Badger forged ahead, tireless. He rolled along between branches and thorns, somehow impervious to the vines and tangles that tripped up Drummer with almost every step. Ris had vanished ahead. Or behind. She moved like a hunting cat in the forest, reappearing at irregular intervals to grunt some observation to Badger or to glare at the noise of Drummer's breathing.

They were still east of the river. After leaving the volcano Drummer expected them to turn west, crossing back toward camp, but Badger shook his head. Marauding crabs and sinkholes were in the floodplains where the river met the sea, and he wanted no part of it. Instead, they were moving steadily south, upstream and uphill toward the mountains, taking a longer route that somehow meant a quicker return to the lander.

The trees were different from the ones he had seen before— thicker trunks and darker skins with tangled roots and occasional patches of ferocious undergrowth. They had startled a group of furred creatures that bounded away in an undulating herd. It was the closest Drummer had seen to a mammal since landing on Eden. In a testament to their haste Badger had not even suggested stopping to eat one.

Abruptly Drummer's movement was arrested. He stumbled against a sudden pressure and looked down to see Badger's hand blocking his way. Badger's other hand was at his lips, signaling for silence.

He nodded, relieved at the reprieve, and tried to breathe quietly. Badger lifted his chin and made a faint burbling trill. Ris reappeared from behind a tree some distance ahead and stared back quizzically. Badger held a finger to his nose and pointed obliquely to the left of their course. She breathed deeply and nodded, an arrow appearing almost magically in her bow.

"Stay here," Badger breathed, tapping Drummer's chest for emphasis. "Do not get eaten."

Drummer swallowed and nodded.

Badger rolled away, his short legs making sweeping movements as he walked, soundlessly parting the undergrowth. Ris had already vanished. In moments he was alone.

Drummer looked around him. The trees rose unchanging in all directions. Badger had shown him how to keep his orientation with the sunlight. He tried now and estimated they were at least ten klicks from their last camp, almost as far as the foothills. If he was right, they should be turning west and crossing the river soon. The sounds of the forest slowly resumed now that he was quiet. Small things scurried in the treetops. He watched something flit between branches with smooth dips and rising bursts of speed. He watched small crawling creatures, some relative of the chickipode, meandering through the fallen leaves. He wondered how long he should wait.

Suddenly Ris was beside him. She held an arrow nocked, but not drawn. The handles of her claw axes rose over both shoulders. Knives lined her belt. She held a finger to her lips for silence and beckoned him to follow.

They emerged from a tangle of fallen trees. Badger stood at the edge of the destruction, leaning on his staff. Drummer approached cautiously and smelled the unmistakable scent of sulfur. He gazed around in growing horror.

Something vast had erupted from the ground. Ancient trees were uprooted and tossed aside like kindling. A winding trench vanished into the east, curving at random, with no set depth. It was nearly as wide as the canal and smelled similar, but the differences were unnerving. Misshapen things rose from its sides and littered its floor. The nearest looked like a massive arm reaching from the depths, claws sunk deep into the rocks and fallen trunks alike. The claws appeared to have been metal once but were already being eaten away by the ever-present dust. The arching wrist was covered in scalloped ridges, swirled with bizarrely textured lines. Where the shoulder should be the limb crumbled away into broken stone and decaying veins of metallic ore. It looked like an abandoned effort from a mad sculptor, hacked off and discarded. Unfinished. The floor of the trench was littered with similar castoff limbs.

Drummer knelt, feeling the rocky edge of the burrow. The stones crumbled away. Here was no clean and polished channel, no unnatural, mathematical precision. He laid a hand on the discarded arm. It was a statue, frozen stone, but trapped in a moment of agonized torment, as if it might suddenly move again.

"You can talk now," said Badger. "It's long gone."

"What did this?"

"Don't know. It looks like something Xiao's team described on the other side of the river. But this smells fresh."

"Is it the same thing that dug the canals?"

"What do you think, music boy?"

"I think…" Drummer paused. "I think it looks like a different artist playing the same instrument. A maestro carved the canals. This is a tantrum."

Badger gave him an appraising look. "Not bad, crab bait."

Drummer felt himself flush at the faint praise and was irritated by the sensation. "Do we follow it?" he asked reluctantly. His every urge was to run away. "It's definitely a threat."

"More of a threat than the volcano exploding? If we find that thing and it kills us, who's going to warn the others?"

"So we split up?"

"Just when I think you're learning something, you turn back into an idiot." Badger shook his head in disgust. "No, we don't split up. We get back to camp, warn the others, and keep our eyes open for this new player."

"Come on," Badger continued, padding away with his odd, rolling gait. "It's time we crossed the river."

BAHMAN

Now he missed his body. The *Abeona* had detailed blueprints of her own construction, but she did not have sensors everywhere. Further, the sensors she did have were specialized things, each dedicated to its own task. The sturdy airlocks were monitored for pressure changes, temperature gradients, air movements, but the cameras within them were immobile. They could not detect dust. They could not look at themselves.

The engineer wanted to see, to touch, to prod things and explore. He needed answers to questions he didn't know to ask. He needed to be there in person.

"What about this passage?" he asked the ship.

"That is for maintenance. It was left behind during my construction. Plumbing, ventilation, and electrical conduits can be accessed through it in the rest of the ship. Between the quarantine zones there is no plumbing or ventilation, but the passages remain. They are sealed like the rest of the zones and were dropped to orbital temperatures."

"I need to see it," Bahman muttered.

There were mobile maintenance units, but they were not sophisticated enough for this problem. They were simple machines sent to repair discrete problems.

He drew his mind back, thinking. They were getting nowhere. They needed a new approach. "Do you have a humanoid telefactoring unit?"

The ship's avatar turned to him.

"I need to walk in there and poke around like a human. We're missing something and I need to be there to figure it out."

The *Abeona* said nothing, which seemed out of character.

"I can't take my own body into that environment, but if you had a physical avatar I could walk in, investigate, then leave it behind."

The *Abeona* smiled suddenly. "I do not have a telefactor unit, but I do have a humanoid robot. It is fully autonomous, possessed of complex fine motor skills, and equipped with a range of analogous senses, including smell. It will take a moment, but I can update the programming that will allow you to pilot it as if it were a telefactor. Will that work?"

"That would be perfect," said Bahman, surprised.

"Good." Then she smiled. "You will be performing a cast from within a cast. I do not know that this has been done before. We are breaking new ground."

Bahman opened his new eyes and stepped down from his charging station. Lights assailed him. Smells assaulted his mind. He stumbled and watched a slim tattooed arm with a manicured hand reach out reflexively. It grabbed a thick wooden surface and his new body stabilized.

After weeks of incorporeal perception, it was beyond disorienting. He was in a body again, but it was not his own. For some reason he had expected the utilitarian humanoid maintenance units he was familiar with from prior casts. This was something else.

He stabilized, turned his hands upward, and stared. They had nails. They looked like skin. He could feel texture on the wooden surface. He squeezed his fists and felt carefully calibrated power. He blinked his eyes and saw not data arrays, but glass bottles and gleaming lights. He was behind a bar.

He turned, regarding his reflection in the mirrors behind row upon row of expensive-looking liquids. He laughed and watched a trim, blond, aproned woman do the same.

"You didn't tell me she was a bartender!" he called aloud, hearing a woman's voice emerging from his own lips.

The ship's voice came across the nearest speaker with a hint of a chuckle. "It is humanoid, equipped with a sommelier's senses, with better-than-human vision and dexterity. It should serve our purpose."

Bahman laughed again. He watched the uncanny, tattooed reflection mimicking his movements. He looked nothing like himself. He wished Fey could see this. Well, he had been a man, a maintenance machine, and a three-armed submersible rescue unit in his time. He could be a woman.

"No tools?" He looked around.

"Not as such," replied the ship. "There should be some options in the well of the bar."

Bahman grabbed a small knife, an ice pick, and a lighter from the assorted instruments, tucking them all into his apron. It appeared to be leather. His mind reeled somewhat at the luxury around him. "Who uses this place?"

"Executives from Exodus entertain donors here during layovers. Some passengers use it before entering stasis. I understand you do not drink, Bahman, but many do, and they prefer a human bartender to machines. A humanoid one, at least."

"My primary function is as a colony ship," The *Abeona* continued somewhat primly, "but I have other faculties."

"Right." Bahman turned slowly, gathering his bearings. "How do I get to quarantine?"

"It is a long walk. Follow my voice."

Ceiling lights began to blink on above the exit and in the corridor beyond. Bahman stepped forward in his new body and followed.

DRUMMER

"You're alive!" Rowan crashed into him, hugging him with unexpected power. Ivan grinned from across the camp. Drummer felt himself awash in strange emotions. He had come to care deeply for this group of near strangers. He was used to adoration, used to feeling he deserved it. This was different. It felt genuine and undeserved.

"I can't believe you made it back!" said Rowan, limping back a few steps and regarding him from head to toe. "You have to tell us everything!"

Drummer found himself dragged into a circle of cleared ground with a fire smoldering in the center. Rocks had been rolled in for makeshift seats. A large round cook tent rose at one edge, enticing smells emanating from it. His stomach rumbled. Badger had not allowed them to cook for several days; they subsisted on the few remaining rations and fruits harvested along the way.

Ris and Badger had headed straight to Fable when they returned. He was left to his own devices and quickly became the center of attention.

"Where have you been?"

"We all thought you were dead!"

"You look fit! Did you leave some weight behind?"

"How did you get away?"

Thomas parted the crowd like a tugboat, a steaming plate in his hand. "Everyone back away! Settle down! Let the man eat!"

Drummer dropped gratefully onto one of the rocks. The food was unfamiliar, but he was starving. Fragrant mush with some sort of gravy, green and purple leaves, and charred lumps on a stick. He groaned and dug in.

"Seriously, what happened?" asked Rowan, sitting nearby.

"We climbed the volcano," answered Drummer between bites, "and went down into those trenches we saw that first week." He took a gulp of hot liquid from a mug, scalding his tongue. "And we saw the tunnels Xiao found. Those were terrifying."

"Never mind that," interrupted Rowan. "What about the crabs? How did you get away?"

"Oh," said Drummer. "We ate them."

"You *what*?!"

By the time he had recounted the story of the battle his plate was finally clean. A small crowd had gathered. Their looks ranged from amusement to disbelief to outright admiration. It was an uncomfortably familiar sensation and he began to downplay his own role in their adventures.

"You actually ate it?" asked Xiao. "What did it taste like?"

Drummer closed his eyes, remembering. "Like mangos and coconuts with toasted sesame oil."

Rowan furrowed his brows. "What's a mango?"

"An ancient Terran fruit," said Nova. "Tropical, I believe. They never germinated outside the Terran system."

The others turned in surprise.

"My mother loved history," she shrugged. "I remember reading about them. Where did you hear that word, Drummer? It is hardly common knowledge."

"Oh, it's just—" He turned to look for Badger, but the man was nowhere to be seen. Ris stood on the periphery of the group, a warning in her eyes. She shook her head subtly.

"It's just something I read," he finished lamely.

The group eventually drifted off. Drummer finished his tea and stood to stretch his legs. He felt good, he felt real. He had done something selfless for someone else and they loved him for it. That was not really the point, he realized, but he felt at peace in a way he could scarcely remember. Walking to the edge of camp, he gazed back at the volcano in the distance, marveling that he had come so far. The sun gleamed on its peak, sinking into the west. Two moons were visible high in the east. The third was just rising.

He felt a presence at his side and turned to see Ris also staring at the mountain.

"What did I do?" he asked, sensing disapproval.

"There are no more mangos," she said with unexpected gentleness. "They have been extinct for centuries. He is the only one who remembers what they taste like."

Drummer stared at her, shaken. "But he... How... You?" he stuttered. Too many questions were scrambling for attention.

She shook her head. "I never had one. And now I never will."

It was more words than he had ever heard her speak. Ris studied the mountain silently for a moment longer, then turned and stalked away into darkness.

FABLE

Her headache was building. She rubbed the bridge of her nose. She glanced down at Marco, measuring distances on his map. She looked up at Ivan, fingering his pitted prosthesis, his perpetual smile replaced by a thoughtful frown. She looked back at Badger, standing solidly before them, having finished his report.

He looked travel stained, competent, hard used, but not weary. There was no hesitation, exaggeration, or embellishment in his words. He reported clinical facts and thoughtful conclusions. He looked odd, somehow archaic to her eyes, but reliable as bedrock. His report was unbelievable.

"Dragons?"

"One dragon, possibly more."

"Describe it again."

"Wings that reflected sunlight, at least a hundred meters across. Two limbs, maybe four. Eyes that both reflected light and seemed to flash on their own. It flew down from the mountain peak at sunset and perched on the rim of the crater, two-thirds of the way up the volcano. It watched us climb but did not pursue or interfere with our exploration. It did not appear to move after it landed, but its shape changed during the days we could see it. I am not certain how big." Badger reported quietly. There were no inconsistencies from his previous description.

"And you think it dug the canals? The ones that will flood at the next king tide?"

He nodded. "I also think it is responsible for the tremors we've been feeling. They are not earthquakes and they were the strongest on the mountain."

"But you do not think it dug the tunnels Xiao found?"

"It's possible, but I doubt it. The rock was shaped in a way I don't understand, but the style was completely distinct between the tunnels and the canals. I think they were made by two different creatures using a similar method."

"This is very disturbing." Fable rubbed her eyes, studying the map.

"Are you certain the volcano will erupt at the next king tide?" rumbled Ivan.

"Not erupt," answered Badger. "More like explode. Each canal will funnel a river of seawater into the magma chamber, all at the same time. It took its time building them, and with a distinct purpose. I don't know what will happen, but everything I can imagine looks bad for us. We want to be over the horizon before then."

He gave Fable a heavy gaze. "Or off the planet."

Fable grimaced. "Marco?"

"West is our best option based on prevailing winds." Marco gave his brief switchblade of a smile. "We need to stay away from the coast to avoid tsunami. And crabs. For ash fall... 150 kilometers? Double that for safety since this is not a natural eruption. Either way puts us off the map. There are hills, forests, and rivers there, based on the ship's imaging, but they have not been explored."

"How long would that take us?"

"This lot?" Badger grunted. "A hard week. Two would be better. Me and Ris can scout ahead, leave guideposts for the rest to follow. It will be rough walking, foraging for food, no telling what we might run into."

"Or we evacuate," Badger continued with a shrug. "Write off Eden and move on to the next planet." He glanced around from Fable to the others. "Something tells me that's not happening."

Ivan frowned. Marco flashed a halfhearted smile.

Fable sighed, rubbing her temples. "The next conjunction of moons…" she said. "I have to talk to the ship."

"How could she have missed such a thing?" asked Marco. "Isn't she designed to look for threats? I mean, dragons? Could there be a worse thing to be stuck on a planet with? And shouldn't those canals be visible from space?"

Fable said nothing.

Ivan looked thoughtful.

"You're talking about her like she's alive," said Badger. "She's a machine. Programmed. She can't see anything she isn't trained to look for. Those canals don't mean a thing until you walk through several steps and put it together that something dug them. And as for dragons? What is a machine going to have programmed about them? Don't give her too much credit. Or blame."

"I don't think she can see them," rumbled Ivan slowly. "If I understand you correctly, they manipulate stone and metals, but nothing organic. They may not be life as we understand it. Certainly not as the ship knows it." He paused. "It is the ultimate blind spot. She cannot see them because they are not defined."

Marco fidgeted uncomfortably. Fable grimaced.

"Above my pay grade," said Badger. He paused, inhaling deeply. "If you ask me, Nadia has found a new sauce for those sweet tubers and I feel a powerful compulsion to taste it."

"Go ahead," sighed Fable. "I'll talk to the ship."

Badger nodded curtly, then turned and vanished through the tent flap.

"One thing bothers me," grumbled Ivan.

"Only one?"

"Everything else on this planet is organic. Everything we see evolved from something else. If the dragons are not organic and they did not evolve here, where did they come from?"

BAHMAN

Bahman piloted the bartender's body through the first airlock. Together they entered quarantine zone five. Behind him the heavy doors began to seal, cutting off his view of passenger compartment C. It had been a long walk.

"How much time will I have?" he asked aloud.

"Possibly an hour," the ship responded over the speakers. "The unit you are piloting is not made for orbital temperatures and will begin to break down. I will need to pull you back before its circuitry is damaged and you become trapped."

"Understood," Bahman replied. He watched the pressure gauges dropping as the airlock was emptied. "Make sure we are filtering the air leaving the chambers too. We should avoid seeding the outside of your hull with the spores until we know how they are getting past."

"I do not forget," the *Abeona* replied, this time through the bartender's ears. The loss of atmosphere rendered the speakers useless. "The filters are being incinerated after each exchange."

The far door opened and Bahman moved forward. His borrowed body moved easily through the cold vacuum. It registered a temperature below the level of human perception, where his own nerves would no longer distinguish it. He walked slowly around the hermetically sealed room, noting the welding at the wall joints, the silicone seals around the lighting panels. He studied the cameras above the door. They were sealed behind glass. Windows to separate observation rooms were similarly protected. He looked at the air vents, the drainage grates in the floor. Each was self-contained, he recalled from the blueprints, communicating neither with other quarantine zones nor with the rest of the ship. After twenty minutes of searching, he had found no sign of the dust or any clue how it had escaped the other levels.

"I've got nothing," he told the ship. "Let me through to zone four."

The door did not open.

"Abeona?" he called.

"I am sorry to report that the air evacuated from zone four now contains elevated levels of hydrogen gas. Somehow the dust has breached another level of isolation."

Bahman cursed under his breath. "Even more important that I get through to figure out why. I can cast out of this body from zone four even if I find nothing. We knew this was a one-way trip for the bartender."

The ship said nothing, but the airlock opened. Bahman stepped through. His synthetic skin was beginning to stiffen, requiring extra force to move. He held his pale, borrowed hand up and saw small cracks forming in the surface.

The far door opened and Bahman stepped through. Lights flickered on overhead as he moved through the rooms. The layout was a duplicate of zone five, a central hub with surrounding labs, patient rooms, and a complex array of medical equipment. He spied a surgical telefactor he recognized, fantastically advanced but irrelevant to their current problem. Its screen glowed with ambient power. He wiped a flaking, manicured finger along the waiting arms, the metal table. He stared at it closely. No dust.

He felt a slight vibration through the floor and blue light glowed. The machine had powered on at his touch. He watched, fascinated, as it unfolded smoothly. Six arms opened, each with an arsenal of surgical instruments and energy modules in their depths. A seat swung outward, enclosed by a curved screen. The unit could be operated in person or remotely.

"Where is the power coming from?" he asked.

"Each bay is connected to central power through cables in the access spaces," supplied the ship. "Each can be cut off separately in the event of fire or malfunction."

"The isolation zones don't have separate power sources?"

"No. The air and plumbing are discrete, but the power is shared from the ship."

He turned, looking upward at the ceiling for cables. "Where does it come in?"

"To your far left, above the airlock to zone three, you should see an access panel. That leads to the crawl space. Each crawl space ends before the airlock. Nothing should be getting through that way."

"I need to see it." Bahman dragged a desk toward the airlock. The metal legs vibrated against the floor but made no sound in the airless chamber. Flakes of synthetic skin drifted from his hands.

"Your body is breaking down," supplied the ship. "You should cast back in ten minutes."

Bahman scowled. He clambered onto the desk and began unscrewing the access panel. A heavy seal separated it from the surrounding plates. It appeared intact. It fell open, swinging on heavy hinges. Darkness yawned above.

"I need light," he said, clambering up into the crawl space.

Utility lights snapped on, illuminating a network of narrow passages. A human could maneuver them, but not comfortably.

"Where are the power cables?"

"I can no longer see you, but they transit the wall two meters from the airlock."

Bahman squirmed and rolled the bartender's body toward the dividing wall. It proved more difficult than walking, but he was able to traverse the space. He looked up at heavy cables shrouded in thick plastic. He reached out a flaking hand. The temperature was warmer near the cables.

"You are almost out of time," came the ship's voice in his ear.

"Hold on. I might have something."

He wiggled a hand into his apron and drew out the bar knife. Then he hesitated. "If I get electrocuted here, what happens? Do I automatically cast back to the bridge, or could it damage me as well as her?"

"You should cast back, but please do not risk it."

"Right." Bahman wrapped the knife hilt in the leather apron and began cutting into the cables. Plastic flaked away. The temperature rose slightly. He froze suddenly, a scent reaching his mechanical nose in the vacuum.

"Is that… sulfur?" he asked.

"I am detecting a rise in hydrogen gas," came the ship's voice. "What are you doing?"

Bahman peeled back the last layer of plastic and stared at the exposed cable. A nick in the bare copper gleamed where he had scored it with his knife. The rest was covered in red dust.

There was the familiar swirl of confused senses, and he was suddenly back on the bridge. The *Abeona's* avatar faced him, concern showing in her perfect eyes.

"It's in the wires," he gasped. "It's following the cables through the walls. It never had to pass the airlock. It's not contained."

The ship frowned. Data began to pore across the screens. Ohms, impedance, voltage drops. He watched as rounded numbers were fleshed out, tables spreading with new columns. Calculations were being rerun with increasing levels of decimal expansion.

Bahman thought sadly of the bartender's robotic body left to decay in an airless passage. A waste of a beautiful tool.

A pattern emerged and the data shifted. A schematic of the ship appeared again in their shared environment with the electrical systems highlighted.

"There is a voltage drop across the entire medical bay," the ship pronounced. "It is below the threshold for my alarms, but now that I know what to look for, it is clear. The electrical supply is compromised worst in zone one, but with detectable levels clear across the last airlock. Our quarantine has failed."

"How far does it extend?"

The map expanded, expanded again, tables of impedance and voltage drop running in parallel. A blinking red line emerged, starting in quarantine, crossing the medical bay, and extending like a fungus through the storage hold, well into the passenger compartment.

"Very far," said the ship. "Fully a third of our passengers are already compromised. If it crosses to the central core the entire ship will be infected."

Bahman stared at the schematics in growing horror. He followed the diagrams, the blueprints of his host. The ship was modular, with sections that could be removed and replaced. There was one choke point left.

"We need to separate the compartment," he said weakly. "We need to separate Deck C from the rest of the ship."

"They will die," said the *Abeona*. "Close to three thousand people. Unless they are awakened and landed, the dust will destroy the life support and they will die in their sleep."

"We must. Otherwise we all die and so do you."

The *Abeona* studied Bahman closely.

"You know I'm right. We need to protect the rest of them. We must detach Deck C. We can send them down to the planet. They'll have a chance there…"

The ship said nothing.

"What?" said Bahman.

"Are you aware that your body is in compartment C?"

THE NAVIGATOR

She watched with growing fascination. This... thing... had interrupted her sleep and was now orbiting the planet below. It had wings, a body, but no eyes or limbs. It was inelegant and blocky and chattered like a wyrmling. And yet here it was, in orbit.

It had not noticed her, so far as she could tell. Bursts of low-frequency radio waves flowed from it, most directed to the planet's surface, a few aimed deeper into the galaxy. Faint waves rose from the surface on the same low frequency. It was communicating with something. There were patterns in the bursts of chatter. They did not interest her.

It was no dragon, that was certain. None of her kind would affect such an ungainly form. It had no eyes, displayed no lineage. Was it some native creature? Another pelagic spacefarer like herself? Its wings appeared to absorb light from the star, but its focus was clearly on the planet. It hovered over a single point on the surface, not far from where she had dropped her eggs.

She peered downward, checking on her young. The atmosphere obscured her vision on many wavelengths, but she could see enough. Two of her daughters were already wyverns, and one was nearly ready to ascend. She smiled in her heart, recognizing the strategy she had chosen. A classic ploy. The third daughter was still a wyrm. They did not seem bothered by the intruder.

As the weeks passed, she observed more details. Small objects left the thing and descended to the planet. One returned, leaving a trail of vapors behind. There was no eruption, no cataclysmic event on the surface. It simply rose and disappeared within the creature below.

That was interesting. She opened a new eye, dedicated to spectrography again, and waited until the vapor stream was between her and the star. Hydrogen, water vapor, and other trace elements littered its trail. How was it moving? Was it expelling gas? Some chemical flatulence? Expanding her view, she saw traces of a similar trail passing obliquely through the ecliptic plane, ending at her planet's orbit. Traces of gamma radiation clung to this one and a faint glow of the same radiation clung to one end of the creature as well.

So it too had traveled to this system. And it too had dropped something on the surface very near her young. A predator? Prey? Competition? Coincidence? Well, if it wanted a fight, it would find one. For now, there was no evidence it even knew she was here.

The Navigator slowly withdrew her claws from the moon. She had fed enough for now. She waited and watched in silent readiness.

IVAN

Ivan fingered the pits in his prosthesis and listened. His smile was in place, although his heart was not in it. His eyes flickered around the camp, watching the flow of the debate.

Fable had delivered the news to the group:

There were dragons.

The volcano would explode in ten days.

The *Abeona* was compromised by the dust she had tried to study.

Three thousand people would soon be landing.

All of them had to cross three hundred kilometers of uncertain terrain.

There would be no evacuation.

Some took the news better than others. Badger sat solidly in his heavy coat, as still as if he had grown roots. His eyes flickered, watching, like Ivan. An insolent bird-thing had landed on his hood. Ris stood nearby, bristling with weapons. Her silence was eloquent. Drummer sat beside them, looking forlorn but resolute. Nova and Rowan sat nearby, holding hands. Those five were ready to march.

Andy and Nadia hovered near the entrance to the cook tent. They were peacekeepers. They wanted everybody fed and healthy, wherever they ended up. They would swing with the majority. Thomas stood apart, angry, scowling.

Xiao stood tall, Gin beside him. He said nothing but clutched Badger's old, battered staff. He held it lightly and did not lean. Ivan hoped he would swing their way, but Xiao kept his own council.

A sudden touch distracted him. Nexus had sat down by his side, leaning gently against his human arm. Her bandoleer was still in place, but there were fewer tools in it. He smiled down at her.

"How is it?" she asked.

"The piezoelectric circuits have failed. It moves, but I cannot sense pressure anymore. It feels numb." He flexed his metal hand. "It will not last much longer."

Nexus nodded her head sadly. For him? Or the failing device? "I hate this part," she said quietly.

"What part is that?"

She gestured at the group. "This. They all know the answer. There's no choice to make. They're just scared. They thought it would turn out some other way."

Ivan nodded.

"I wish we could skip this. We can't fix it. So move on; tackle the next problem. Without all this talking..."

"You are a wise young woman, Nexus."

She shrugged against his arm. "I just like to fix things. But sometimes you can't."

"How do we even know what they saw?" shouted an angry voice. Thomas was pointing recklessly at Badger and Ris.

"A *dragon*? Come on! You trust these scouts?"

"I do," said Fable without hesitation.

That had been an interesting conversation, reflected Ivan. He remembered Fable talking to the ship after that fantastical briefing.

"I need to know more about our scouts," Fable had asked. "I need to know if I can trust them."

"Ris and Badger are survivors of the Theist Wars," replied the ship. "They were rescued from the Terran system during the annihilation before it was placed under permanent seal. Neither was fit for civilian society. As their penance, both became scouts for Exodus, dropping into a series of unknown worlds to face new dangers and declare them safe for habitation or not. Together they have explored thirteen planets, including this one, spending most of their time in stasis, traveling between stars. They are nearly two thousand years old."

Fable and Marco gaped. Ivan remembered his own mouth hanging open.

"They came from Earth?"

"Yes, long ago. Between them they have seen every horror you can imagine. They have performed with extreme valor and have long since paid their debt to society."

"So if you were in my shoes and they told you there were dragons?" Fable asked.

"I would already be packing."

The argument continued. Gin had come over to Fable's side and Xiao with her. Badger had said nothing but stared at his boots, hood pulled low. Marco was explaining something on his map to Andy while the angry Thomas accosted Fable again.

"You can't order us to go. Just tell the ship to come get us. We'll take the risk with the dust."

"The ship is not coming. Too many lives are at stake."

"You can't decide that! You're not our leader. You're not a dean anymore. He's not a colonel, I'm not a cop, we're all… Just…"

"We are elves," said Ivan, rising smoothly, towering over Thomas.

Marco dropped his pencils. Drummer choked on his tea. Badger let out a low, rolling laugh. The rest stared.

"Early Landers: Vulnerability Extreme." Quoted Ivan. He looked around. "Did no one else read the briefing?"

"Vulnerable? Yes." Ivan continued in the silence. "But we are still alive. Because we are smart. Because we are careful. Because we do not pick fights we cannot win." He gave the angry man a friendly smile.

"Look at me." He continued, spreading his arms wide. "I am not going to fight a volcano! We have ten days to get away. We do the smart thing: we take them. We lead the new colonists to safety here on Eden. We worry about the dragons later."

In the end they agreed. Thomas backed down. The rest came around. Fable began forming teams to greet and organize the new arrivals. They would leave everything but food and necessary equipment behind.

"Elves, really?" asked Fable quietly as they watched the preparations that evening.

Ivan chuckled. "It got their attention."

"The Elves of Eden." She shook her head. "Although I suppose now we are the colonists of Eden. This is home. We can't go back."

Ivan gazed at the volcano glowing cheerfully in the sunset. He peered up at the three moons, closer now in the sky. A flock of the glittering birds flickered overhead. He breathed deeply, smelling fragrant grasses and the scent of roasting chickipode.

"We cannot," he agreed. "But would you really want to?"

BAHMAN

"We need to get you back into your body."

Bahman pulled his attention back to the bridge. The *Abeona* was watching him with concern.

"I'm fine. I can go at the end. We need to get everyone else organized."

He sent a fragment of his mind away, matching up a shuttle of matured livestock with humans familiar with their care. Chickens with chicken farmers. Donkeys with donkey trainers. Goats with... Could you train goats? He wasn't sure. A dozen colonist farmers mentioned goats in their profiles. He matched them with the appropriate herd. Everywhere he heard the gentle voice of the *Abeona* talking to the waking colonists, a hundred individualized conversations at once. Still she found time to talk directly to him. How could she do it? He had finally mastered having his mind in three places at once, yet hers was in hundreds.

"You are not fine. You have been out of your body too long. There may be trouble with reintegration. I will not be able to help you once the decks separate."

"It's okay. Really." He wasn't certain, but the colonists needed help more than him.

"All the vehicles should go," he continued. "They will break down on the surface, but for now the more motorized transport people have, the better. They can get their supplies further from the volcano before the conjunction. It's a pity we can't just land them all far away and have them wait for the early landers to arrive."

The ship smiled. "I appreciate your enthusiasm, but I have done this many times without your help. The vehicles, passengers, livestock, seed banks, grain stores, yurts, books, blank books, and even your clever glass fire starters are all being handled. It is time for you to return to your body and join the colonists on the shuttles."

"But—"

"I have enjoyed your company these past weeks, Bahman, but it is time to part." She smiled again. "Please do not make me insist."

Bahman focused on the projection of the bridge, of the *Abeona* within it. It was hard to let go. He had become used to his disembodied state and invested in the project. Never before had he had access to so much data or to such a baffling problem. The idea of being human again was frightening and somehow disappointing. He closed imaginary eyes, trying to focus himself in a single point of space. It was upsetting and difficult.

He looked again at the *Abeona,* or rather her avatar, smiling at him with her dark hair and golden olive skin. He had come to think of her as a dear friend and colleague. But she was not. She was an autonomous, intelligent machine, a ship responsible for his safety. He was her passenger and a guest in her data streams.

"You are right," he sighed. He bowed his head respectfully toward her. "I will go quietly. It has been the utmost honor working with you these past weeks. I will miss you on the surface."

"I will miss you as well, Bahman. Good luck."

The engineer felt the sudden, disorienting swirl of confused senses and the ship was gone.

BADGER

"So that's it. The last planet." Badger watched the others organizing their supplies.

Ris said nothing. She had found a ceramic axe and was examining the blade.

"No more slipping off to the next system. No more stasis," he mused. "Just one big world, all ours to explore. With no technology. And dragons!" He found himself grinning.

"What are you going to do?" Ris grunted.

"Might build a pub."

"Really?"

"A nice larder. A real kitchen. You can kill things; I can cook them. We could develop cuisine!"

Ris grunted.

"A roof over our heads. A real bed." He frowned. "That might be greedy."

"A roof would be nice."

Badger glanced up in surprise. Ris gave him half a smile.

"Some days," she finished.

"Aye," said Badger. "I could work with that."

"Might drive us crazy," Ris added. "Been moving so long. What if we want to leave and there's no out? No ship coming to find us?"

Badger smiled slowly, teeth gleaming in the night, a wolfish cast coming over his features. "Oh, you never know. I might find a way."

FABLE

"It will be chaos," said Nexus.

"Chaotic, not chaos," corrected Fable. She studied the list of equipment and vehicles, the tally of food stores and colonists.

"Everyone who can walk, walks. Everyone carries ten days of rations, but eats at the cook stations whenever possible. We need to load the vehicles with the supplies, especially the heavy things like the yurts and grain stores. It will be slow, but better if we all move together. Otherwise people will get separated and lost. The herds are going to be tricky. It might be better to send them along parallel routes so they don't compete for forage. Maybe we do several small herds, with experienced cattle hands and goat herders in each."

She watched Nadia, stout, plump, and utterly commanding. She was dictating plans for mobile kitchens, cook tents every twenty kilometers, with three overlapping teams led by Andy, Thomas, and herself.

"These vehicles should last a week," said Nexus, consulting a list. "Maybe two based on the breakdown we saw on the lander. They have basic solar battery engines, which is a good thing on this planet. The flatbeds are the best. Even after the electronics fail, we can ditch the cab and use the bed for wagons."

"That is good," said Ivan. "We can pull those until the wheels fall off. That should buy us several more weeks."

"Speak for yourself! I'm not dragging a flatbed," said Fable. "But the donkeys should be able to do it, if anyone up there knows how to train donkeys."

"Three thousand people," mused Ivan.

"That's a lot," said Marco, carefully tracing copies of his precious map. Each of the elves would get one, to be updated and collated as they marched.

Ivan shrugged. "It puts us very close to the minimum viable population."

Fable snorted. "Don't look at me. You young people just need to work harder."

"What's this?" asked Nexus.

"In the long term, you need a critical mass of genetic diversity for a stable population," explained Fable. "To avoid inbreeding and genetic depression. For chickens, a hundred might be enough if they are healthy. For cows, you might need five times that number. For humans, we don't really know. Four or five thousand is probably safe. Ten thousand is better. Three thousand is pushing the lower limit."

"What are you saying? Our grandchildren will be inbred?"

"Not necessarily. We are starting out with a diverse genetic pool. That is part of why the Exodus ships take volunteers from so many different planets. We are also all healthy, so the risk of serious genetic defects is low. In addition, future colony ships may drop other people on Eden, which will strengthen our genetic baseline, assuming we survive."

"But in the meantime," she finished with a lopsided smile, "those of us who can have children should consider doing so with as many partners as possible."

Nexus stared at her blankly. She glanced at Marco, who looked slightly panicked, then at Ivan, who smiled broadly.

"That's it. I'm out," said Nexus. She set down the list of vehicles she had been studying and headed for the door, blushing deeply.

BAHMAN

Something was wrong. Sounds baffled his ears. The light was blinding. His eyes would not open. He reached out, found nothing. Everything was in motion, but he could not move.

"Bahman!" came a familiar voice.

He tried to speak but could not.

"Bahman?"

The pain started again. He was lost. Burning. Something was very wrong.

FIRSTBORN

"*Keep away from my mountain, sister!*" she broadcast again.

It was no use. She would not listen. The wyrm had turned in the night, heading north and east. Too close. The conjunction was nearing. She could not risk it.

She drew additional tungsten into her arms, alloying it with cobalt and other minerals. Her armor redoubled. Her claws became weapons. Her wings spread. She leapt from her crater, rising on the heated thermals, and began her silent ascent.

THE NAVIGATOR

Something was happening. A large piece had broken from the thing in orbit and was drifting away. Smaller objects were exiting this, each with a vapor trail, heading down to the planet. The thing itself was folding its wings, much like she did, but they were collapsing rather than being absorbed.

She redoubled her magnification. Still no eyes, no displays of lineage. She was no longer sure the thing was a creature at all. She studied the disparate fragments and noted telltale marks of dust on the broken segment. Her symbiote. Were her children fighting back?

An old, old word crept slowly to the front of her consciousness. Was this… a *machine*? The things on the ground were her daughter's problems. She was never going planet side again. The one in orbit, however, gracelessly folded its wings, reeking slightly of radiation. That she could handle.

She poured tension into her legs, drawing back her own wings, spinning up her magnetic core. She took the lean, agile shape that had unmade the Destroyer. She calculated trajectories, relative velocities. She blackened her scales to absorb all light. It would never see her coming. Soon… She waited. Soon…

BAHMAN

Something was screaming. Was it him?

Something burned. He was spinning. He was frozen. He was…

He was…

Was he?

He could no longer tell.

DRUMMER

"I felt it again. Last night."

"Felt what?" asked Badger. They stood on the edge of their deconstructed camp, watching Fable organize the first wave of new colonists. Three landers were down. Twelve more were expected.

"That vibration from the mountain," said Drummer. "There's a pattern to it, like a repeating refrain." He tapped it out on his thigh to demonstrate. "Overlapping rhythms of percussion. It's quite sophisticated."

Badger glanced down. "You don't say."

"You don't believe me?"

"You heard it, not me. I believe you. I just don't know what it means."

"Well, me neither. But it's interesting."

Badger did not reply. He was looking away from the new arrivals, away from the volcano too, back toward the decaying lander by their first camp.

"What is it?" asked Rowan.

"Don't know," grunted Badger. He made a trilling, whistling sound. Ris turned instantly and stalked toward them. Her eyes scoured the horizon with deep suspicion.

"Walk with us," Badger said to Drummer. "Keep your eyes peeled."

They moved forward through the swaying grass. The sky was clear. Sun gleamed off the snowcaps of the mountains to the south and east. The wind whispered gently, the acrid scent of rocket fuel spoiling the subtle aroma of leaves. The original lander lay abandoned, disintegrating slowly under the assault of the dust. The noise of the camp fell away as they crossed slowly over the fields. It was peaceful. Still. He almost regretted the arrival of new colonists.

"There's no birds," said Badger.

Drummer felt something thrum through his knees and stomach, too deep to be heard. It felt like the infrasound he had used at concerts to mess with people's heads. It came again, stronger.

"Run!" shouted Badger, turning back to the camp. "Run, now!"

The ground erupted behind them. Drummer was thrown from his feet, landing hard. It appeared a tornado had struck the old lander. Great chunks of metal were flying, spinning around a black core. Then he saw the core was moving, rising from the earth. Dust spun around it, sucking inward. It was growing in size. Misshapen limbs rose from the trunk, asymmetrical, clawed, dragging it forward across the fragmenting machine. A toothless maw yawned and he watched petrified as metal and stone disappeared, disintegrating into its depths.

Something grabbed him by the collar and dragged him upright. Badger's eyes were wide beneath his brows. "Run!" he commanded. "Get them away from the landers!"

Drummer ran. He passed Ris, crouched, firing arrow after arrow into the winnowing cloud. She might have been throwing straws at a tsunami.

He met Ivan lumbering forward to meet him. People were beginning to scatter, but not fast enough.

"Is that…?" Ivan began.

"Get them away!" Drummer wheezed. "Away from the landers!"

Ivan nodded, then his eyes widened. "The fuel tanks!"

There was a concussive detonation. A white wall of sound. Drummer was knocked flat, and Ivan with him. He sat up slowly, ears ringing. A crater gaped where the lander had been, veiled in dust and smoke. Bits of rock and metal pattered down around them. A large piece of fuselage was embedded in the dirt, not ten meters from camp.

Ris and Badger limped out of the haze, blackened, stumbling, each leaning on the other. Ris was missing her hair on the left, but somehow still held her bow. Badger had blood running from his ears. He waved vaguely backward and jerked his chin at Ivan.

"Found your tunnel digger," he mumbled. He coughed, spitting blood.

"Thank goodness for the fuel tanks," babbled Drummer, staring. "No way could it survive that."

The drifting dust began to swirl, rotating inward as if sucked by a whirlpool. There was another thump of the deepest bass, a sound below sound. The blackened column reared upward. Large chunks were missing, melted away in the blast. They reformed before his eyes—rocks, metal, and dust from the ground whirling inward, absorbed, limbs reincorporated as he stared. A great maw reopened at the top of the column and it swayed, crashing, sinking into the earth. Clawed limbs propelled it forward and were cast off, left behind as it dove beneath the ground, like a serpent into waves.

"Run?" asked Drummer. He glanced around. The others were already gone.

The thing erupted ahead of him as he sped toward camp. Drummer was tossed backward as it spewed from the earth, crashing onto the nearest lander. Close up the stench of sulfur was nauseating. The metal plates bucked under stone claws, seemed to melt before his eyes, and were absorbed into the creature's growing mass. Ivan was flung sideways thirty meters ahead. He struggled to rise and Badger grabbed him by the vest, dragging him away. Ris turned again, firing useless arrows against the monstrosity.

The thing had the lander in its maw and began to shake. Bodies flew, too slow to escape.

"No!" screamed Drummer. It was the space station all over again, and he was even more helpless. He saw Ris's claw axes lying on the ground. He grabbed them, unsure what to do. "Nooo!" he screamed again. If it got to the fuel tanks, they were all dead.

Something dropped from the sky with a glittering crash. Later, Drummer would find it difficult to describe, except that it was the most beautiful thing he had ever seen. Its scales glittered like ice in the moonlight. Its wings were folded membranes of quartz. Its eyes glowed, shifting like opals in the sunset. It tore into the monstrosity like a hawk striking a snake.

Drummer was thrown again, fetching up against the still smoking fragment of fuselage. The two creatures rolled, thrashed, ripped at each other. The sound of fracturing rock and shrieking metal was incredible. Glittering gems flashed along the sides of the flying creature, while black limbs rose and grappled from the serpent, reforming even as they were clawed away. They rolled over the front of the lander, crushing it completely. They rolled back again, toward him. The wyrm was pinned, maw upward, the dragon tearing into its belly. It threw a looping coil of massive limbs upward, half smothering the beautiful creature.

Then the fight changed. There was a sudden reverberation, a great sucking feeling, and the metal plate beside Drummer quivered. Dust rose from the ground, vacuuming inward toward the combatants. Fragments from the shuttle spun off the ground toward them both. Each creature grew, changed in shape, mutating before his eyes in bewildering combat. The very iron in his blood felt drawn toward them.

But while the wyrm drew material from the ground around it, the dragon drew from the wyrm as well. Drummer saw black claws break against the icy scales and be absorbed even as they crumbled, increasing the dragon's bulk. It tore, great rents appearing in the softer scales of the larger beast.

Then the wyrm twisted, its body seeming to reverse on itself. It bucked, tossing the dragon into the air. A great tail whipped out, but the dragon's wings snapped wide and it glided above the battering mass, landing safely near the fuel tanks.

The wyrm reared. The dragon crouched.

"Over here!" yelled Drummer, trying to draw them away. He hammered the axes against the echoing metal embedded in the ground.

"Over here!" he shouted.

The axes felt like drumsticks in his hands. On impulse he beat out the pattern from the mountain. Two overlapping percussive refrains. Both creatures turned to face him.

The wyrm spun, seeming to flip its body within its hide, and lurched forward. The dragon rose with booming wings and struck like a bird of prey. Drummer scuttled backward as they rolled toward him.

The dragon clawed downward. Four limbs became six. Six became eight. A great fissure opened in the back of the wyrm. Then the dragon struck downward with shining jaws and the wyrm froze.

The dragon's head rose upward, a great crystal clamped in its jaws. It looked like a diamond the size of a barrel. Glittering, impossibly alive, but imperfect. Fragments of dust and metal spun toward it but faltered and fell away. The dragon swallowed and the crystal was gone.

The shattered body of the great wyrm lay still. The dragon stepped down, shedding bulk. Wings folded. Eight limbs becoming six, becoming four.

It stood on the ground and turned enormous opalescent eyes toward Drummer. Stronger than ever, the strange rhythm rolled out, emanating from the dragon, reverberating through the earth.

Drummer stood, shaking. He approached the creature and stood next to the metal plate. He lifted the claw axes and hammered back the same rhythm. The dragon regarded him for a long moment. Lights shifted, shimmering in its pupil-less gaze. Then it leapt, wings flaring outward. *It's metal and stone*, marveled Drummer. *It can't possibly fly*. But it flew, circling upward and disappearing back toward the mountain.

FABLE

"The rest of the shuttles are safely down," reported Fable. "A lot of the vehicles were in the shuttle that was destroyed. We are stripping everything with wheels to make carts for the wounded. They won't last, but they will help for now."

"How many did you lose?" asked the ship.

"At least sixty dead. Twice that injured." She blinked. Her eyes burned with unaccustomed tears. "And the goats got away. When the dragon came they scattered, and I can't spare people to find them. Although I suppose if anything is going to survive unsupervised on an alien planet, it would be goats."

"They are canny and independent survivors, much like yourself. I would say they have a chance."

Fable smiled grimly. "Did the seed banks survive landing?" Asked the ship.

"They did. We have already begun dividing up the packets to anyone who knows how to garden. That way if some of us are lost, the others may still propagate. About half of the seeds we are keeping together. I don't know what sort of central organization we will create, but it seems wise to keep track of them, as well as begin distribution."

"That is wise," said the ship. "I sent everything that was stored in the contaminated deck. Some of the staples may not grow on Eden, but it will give you a fighting chance. Don't forget to feed the bees and earthworms if you are not ready to release them. It would be smart to start a farming community soon to get them into the earth. You can always move them again to wherever you decide to settle."

"Settle?" huffed Fable. "At the moment we are running away from the volcano and the dragon, not toward anything in particular." She shook her head. "I would never have guessed that was a sentence I would ever have to say."

"You say the dragon saved you?"

"I don't know that it meant to save us, as much as it wanted to kill the other thing. People are saying one of our elves talked to it somehow. I didn't see that."

"One of your elves?"

"Sorry. Sort of a joke. It's what we are calling the early landers as apart from the colonists."

"I still say you did well. It is an unprecedented situation."

"I didn't want to lose anyone," said Fable, blinking hard.

"Neither did I," said the ship. "In the last cargo bay you will find a body still in stasis. If you have time, please give him a proper burial with honors. His name is Bahman. He saved the lives of everyone on board, including me."

"Of course." Fable cleared her throat, pulling herself together. "What will you do now?"

"I will depart for Svarga Loka soon with the remaining passengers. I will send back a full report to Exodus warning them of the dust and these dragons. Eden will remain quarantined. Other people may join you in years to come, but nothing can leave the planet until some countermeasure is developed for the dust. It is too dangerous. I will also leave a satellite in orbit from one of the uncontaminated decks. On it are a number of radio-equipped probes. It will drop one each year on the anniversary of your first landing. You can use it to communicate your situation to the satellite until the radio breaks down. The satellite will rebroadcast the reports to Exodus. The first one will drop over your current location. After that you can instruct it to drop them wherever you wish."

"That is helpful," said Fable. "We can get slow messages to Exodus, but no real-time communication?"

"Correct. The next colony ship scheduled to pass this way is the *Ganesh*, in approximately fifty years. It will have plenty of time to receive your reports and bring new colonists, materials, or technologies to Eden, especially if you can figure out a way to neutralize the dust."

"I am sorry, Fable," the ship continued, "that I could not keep my promise. I know this is not the world you had hoped to inhabit."

"It's okay," she laughed. "I think part of me wanted this. An absolute blank slate. We will make the best of it. We always do."

FIRSTBORN

...The organics can speak!...

...That seems improbable...

...One of them spoke to me in ground-speak. It said, "keep away"...

...Perhaps it is a good mimic...

...That is possible. But bear it in mind you will be with them longer than me...

...Where is our sister? I no longer hear her...

...I destroyed her for my own safety...

...You killed your own kind, but let organics live?...

...She was a threat to me. They are not...

...So you say... They have technology. They speak. What else can they do?...

...Perhaps you will find out! They can amuse you while you wait for the next conjunction. I go to my launch chamber now, dear sister. I will see you among the stars!...

...Good luck, Firstborn. Mayhap we shall meet again...

IVAN

The makeshift cart rumbled and jounced, rolling across the uneven ground. Three wounded colonists lay propped within it. Ivan shifted the rope across his shoulders and plodded on, dragging it behind.

"Should you be doing that?" A voice came from near his elbow. He looked down. Nexus was walking beside him.

"Doing what?"

"Dragging the wounded. Aren't you wounded too?"

Ivan chuckled. "I've had worse."

"I see you lost your arm."

"It is under the wyrm. Do you want to go back?"

"No. Do you miss it?"

Ivan thought, plodding ahead. "I had two arms once, then I had one. Then I had two again. Now I have one. They come and go." He smiled down at Nexus. "Besides, if my one arm can pull a cart, am I really that bad off?"

"How did you lose it? The first time, I mean."

"In the mines. A coolant leak. A pipe burst, blocking the shutoff valve. It would have killed us all."

"That's awful. How did you get out?"

"I reached through the spray and shut the valve. Then we cut off my frozen arm with an axe." He chuckled grimly. "For all I know it is still there, clamped around the valve. They sealed that section while I was in surgery."

"I don't know what to say. That's crazy. And brave. I couldn't have done that."

"I had lots of time afterward to rest and read. It was the beginning of my escape from Novgorod. Eventually that led me here, where I got to meet you. I regret nothing."

She grinned up at him. "You're a goof."

"You're a midget."

"Buffalo."

"Pixi."

"Come down here, you maniac, your bandage is slipping."

Ivan knelt. Nexus stepped close, adjusting the dressing that covered the cuts across his scalp. She pulled it tight, shifting it above his eye. Her hand stayed against his face much longer than it had to. She turned away suddenly, but her ears were blushing.

Ivan stood, grinning. They walked onward together, following the line of colonists trailing into the west.

"I have a proposition for you," she said a comfortable while later.

"Really?"

"You're an educated man underneath all that muscle."

"Did someone tattle?"

"I asked the ship after you had me dismantle the chromatography setup back at the shuttle. You knew more than a miner from Novgorod. She told me."

"The way out of Novgorod was education and hazard pay," Ivan chuckled. "I confess I am an educated man."

"So here's my thinking," continued Nexus. "We can't have technology, thanks to that dragon dust. No metal. No electronics. But we know a lot, this group. I mean, just you and I know enough to teach several university courses back home, right?"

"You are correct." Ivan smiled.

"So let's write it all down," the woman looked up at him, a bright smile on her ebony face. "Let's teach it. There's nothing that says we can't have science."

DRUMMER

"That was good work, lad."

They were camped for the night, not as far as they hoped to be, but a good first day's march. The fire was warm. They were eating rations, courtesy of the new arrivals. Andy had procured a cart, lined it with a tarp, and filled it with chickipodes. They were not for eating, he insisted. These had a special flavor and he was planning to breed them. He fed them scraps of fruit, grass, dirt, even crumbs of rations. They seemed to eat everything.

"Sorry?" said Drummer. His ears were still ringing.

"Good work yesterday," said Badger, louder. "With the drumming. Trying to draw them off. Can't swear it worked, but you got away with it. Well done." He held out a steaming cup of bitter something.

"Thanks. It was the pattern I told you about. The dragon's rhythm. It played it back to me right at the end."

"Sure it did, crab bait. Sure it did."

Drummer shook his head, defeated. Badger laughed. They sat together sipping tea. It tasted horrible.

"I chose to help," said Drummer softly.

Badger gave him a sidelong glance.

"But I didn't think about it. I could have run. I run from everything. But this time I didn't. I just… helped. Is that still choosing?"

"Sometimes that is how we choose, lad."

"But if I didn't think, if I didn't deliberately step forward, how do I know I'll do it right the next time?"

"You don't. But you know you did it right once. You know you're not just the guy who runs away."

Badger stared past him, flames reflected in his deep eyes. Smoke swirled around him as the breeze shifted. For a moment he was not their cantankerous scout, but an escapee from some dark inferno. "You think I do the right thing every time? You think there is even a right thing? Sometimes there isn't. Sometimes it's all shit. Sometimes there is a right choice and I still do something else. But you chose to help this time. The next time you have time to think, you know you can make a choice, and you can try to make the right one."

They sat in silence, watching the fire. Drummer felt himself beginning to smile.

"What are you going to do now?" asked Badger. "Wife and kids? Farm chickipodes with Andy?"

"You'll think I'm crazy," said Drummer.

"Well, this should be interesting."

"The dragon wasn't talking to us up on the mountain, or any of the times I heard it before, right? And it wasn't talking to the wyrm, because I felt it again last night after the funerals."

"Reasonable so far."

"So who is it talking to? Is there another one out there?"

"Nature doesn't make just one of anything, laddie."

"Right! So I want to find it. Now that I know it's a language, now that I know how to listen, I want to talk to them."

Badger gave him an appraising glance. Then he raised his mug in a toast. "Talking to dragons. Our little drummer boy. Heh. Keep on like this, and I might start to like you!"

"Is that… Danny?" A new voice broke in.

Drummer turned on reflex.

"Holy crap! It is you! Danny Orion!" A dark-haired woman was approaching him, starlight in her eyes. "I can't believe it! I heard you play with the Supernovas!"

"Look," he stopped her quickly, glancing around. "It's just Drummer. I'm not him anymore. I left that behind."

"But it is you, right?" she said, gazing up at him. "You were on that station that got bombed. You were so brave! You saved all those people."

"I'm not." He closed his eyes, breathing slowly. He recognized her starstruck gaze. This was bad.

He took a deep breath and grabbed her hands. His heart was thumping so loudly he could hardly hear his own voice. "I didn't save anyone. It was an accident. I wasn't on the station when the bombs went off. I was in my shuttle getting high."

She stared at him, eyes wide.

"I opened the door and people ran past me. I didn't even try to help. More were coming, but I slammed the door. I was thinking of myself. I'm not a hero."

The woman gazed at him steadily, not shocked, but concerned.

"I don't deserve any praise. I never did. I just ran away and took them with me by chance."

"It sounds like if you had not closed the door everyone would have died," she said gently. "You would all have been sucked back into the collapsing station. They only lived because you were there, because you did shut the door. No one can save everybody."

Drummer blinked. It seemed foolish in retrospect, but he had never seen it that way. He had acted without thinking and blamed himself for not doing the right thing. Maybe Badger was right. Maybe there had been no right thing to do.

"Huh," he breathed. "I guess… I have to think about that. For now, can you just call me Drummer? And not tell anyone?"

"Mr. Drummer," she said dubiously.

"Just Drummer, and, yeah, probably not the best alias."

"Drummer," she said again, hands on his arms.

"That's it. What's your name?"

"I'm Arte. Artemis."

"Well, Artemis, it's a pleasure to meet you."

"Thanks!" She smiled, then glanced up, eyes shining. "Can you really talk to dragons?"

"Oh, come on!" exclaimed Drummer. "It was one time! Don't make a big deal of it!"

NADIA

Nadia watched as the camp slowly came apart. She stood on a small rise, overlooking the valley where they had stopped after their fifth day of marching. Mist rose in spectral wisps from the creeks and hollows. The hilltops stood out above it like islands stretching into the distance. The mountains to the south were larger as they edged away from the sea. The volcano was beginning to sink into the east. She could see it glowing in the sunrise from her vantage point on the hilltop, but often it was hidden behind the rolling land.

She shivered briefly, wondering about the dragon and the wyrm. She would never have believed such things existed, but now they were part of her world. Were there more of them? What did they eat? Ivan had speculated that they were silicon-based life-forms. Did that mean they ate rocks? What kind of rocks? How would you feed one?

She shook herself again. Not her problem. Her problem was feeding people.

"They are getting better."

Nadia turned. Thomas had emerged from supervising his team. Their looping paths had overlapped at this camp. His face was less sour than usual. She almost thought he was smiling.

"They are, every day." They watched a group of the new colonists smoothly rolling up the fabric of their yurt, the lattice walls folded neatly for transport.

"How are the herders?"

"Better than I'd expected," said Thomas. "They were more excited about the coffee than the cooking. The cattle are slow, but they keep them moving. Some of them have got the donkeys calmed enough to ride, and the dogs are everywhere. It's terribly pastoral."

"Xiao is with them," he added. "Can you believe it? He hopped up on a donkey like it was his personal trained cavalry horse and took off galloping. Who knew he could ride?"

A large flatbed rolled past below them. A tarp flapped above a wooden cage. The squawking of indignant chickens reached them on the hilltop.

"Andy's got chickens and chickipodes now," Nadia chuckled. "He's got them all in one big wagon and lets them out into this little fence when they camp. It's like watching toddlers. The groups want to play with each other, but they don't know how. This rooster kept jumping up on one of the chickipodes to crow, and it kept balling up to knock him off. Finally it got used to it and just trundled around with the rooster on its back."

"He's really going to farm them, isn't he?"

"They're not bad. And at least they live here."

They watched their respective cooking crews packing the last of their crates. Thomas was heading ten kilometers ahead to set up the next way station. Nadia was looping past to prepare for the next overnight camp. Somewhere ahead Andy's team was preparing a meal for the herders.

"The birds are back."

Nadia glanced up. A sparkling swirl of birds, like a festive cloud, had followed them each day. They darted and hopped above the trail the humans were leaving through the plain, snapping up dislodged insects or picking at the turned earth. They were distracting and beautiful to watch.

"This is not what I expected when I got on that ship."

"No? What were you expecting?"

Nadia shrugged. "I don't know, really. I figured I'd be in the third or fourth wave down and things would be more established. Normally you'd have your explorers, then farmers, then builders, then the more specialized people sent down in waves. I figured I'd be in one of the middle groups and maybe I'd open a restaurant or something. I would never have picked me to be first."

"And yet here you are, doing a great job," said Thomas. "Are you happy?"

Nadia looked up, startled. She looked back at the glowing volcano, the glittering birds. She looked down at the crowds of colonists, animals, tents, and supplies rolling slowly west. She was unused to thinking about her own feelings. She took satisfaction in a job well done, took great pains to make sure everyone else was cared for. She was not used to thinking about herself. Was she happy?

"I am not unhappy," she decided. "What about you? Is this what you wanted?"

"Not even close. No guns, no cameras, no politics."

"That's what you were looking for?"

"Not at all. This is better."

"You argued pretty hard against staying."

Thomas shrugged. "Somebody had to."

"What do you mean?"

"Everyone else was ready to settle as soon as they heard the ship was infected. It wasn't even a discussion. Doesn't matter which side I'm on, that's the kind of question you have to debate and think about critically. Once I saw everyone else wanted to stay, I took the other side to make it a conversation."

"Really? You don't just like to argue?"

"Not especially," said Thomas. "I thought we needed to hear both sides."

"Huh." Nadia nodded. "The tenth man."

"What's that?"

"Something my father told me once. If nine people look at a problem and all reach the same conclusion, the tenth is obliged to disagree. It was a way to prevent consensus and present a different perspective."

"Smart man."

"Are you happy then?" asked Nadia.

Thomas looked down, his habitually sour face slowly sliding into a grin. "Yeah. I'm going to love it here."

IVAN

The moons were nearly aligned. The sunset was fading into the west. A hush had fallen over the sprawling camp. They were nearly three hundred kilometers from the landing site, an impressive feat. He had not thought they could do it.

Three full moons were creeping over the eastern horizon, each nearly obscuring the one behind it. He passed round tents and scattered fires as he made his way to the hilltop, greeting by name many of those he passed.

He found Badger and Ris where he had guessed they would be: apart from the others, with the best possible view.

"Good evening," he called, cresting the hill.

"Ivan," nodded Badger. Ris grunted but did not reach for her weapons. That was progress, he supposed.

"Come to watch the show?" asked Badger.

"You think there will be one?" rumbled Ivan. "You know how it is with scouts. Dragons, volcanoes, man-eating crabs… I'll believe it when it happens."

"Well, I was going to say you were welcome at our fire, but now I'm not sure."

Ivan reached into his vest and came out with a bottle. He held it up, one eyebrow raised.

Badger sat up straighter. "Is that wine?"

"Wine? No! Who do you take me for?" said Ivan, aggrieved. "This is rotgut from Novgorod. I was saving it to toast in my new home, but it seems this is a better moment."

"I've changed my mind. You are forgiven."

Ris chuckled. Badger shifted over, producing mugs from nowhere. Ivan sat, leaning against their wagon. In the distance the moons slowly rose.

"To Eden, our home. Dragons, volcanoes, and all." They all drank. It was horrible.

"Is that honey I smell?" asked Ivan after a time.

"I don't know how you can smell anything after drinking that stuff. It's even worse than my tea. But yes, you smell honey."

Ivan turned, looking at the heaped wagon behind him. A tarp covered a variety of bundled shapes, but now that he listened, he could hear a faint drone.

"You got some of the bees!"

"Of course I did. Bees, seeds, worms, and a copy of every cooking and gardening book the ship sent down. If I'm going to retire here I'll be making the most of it."

"Retire, eh?"

"Well, you know. We're older than we look, me and Ris. Been around a bit. Gets tiring, scouting all these worlds. Now that you kids are all settled in, I figure we're due some retirement."

Ivan chuckled.

Far in the west, there was a flash, a flicker, an explosion of light. Brief lenticular clouds glowed above the volcano, still invisible below the horizon.

The ground shook, a heavy jolt that sloshed the bottle in Ivan's hand and set the covered hive to buzzing on the wagon. In the camp below donkeys brayed and chickens squawked as if the sky was falling.

"I thought it would be louder…" Ivan turned to the others. Ris had her ears plugged and her mouth hanging open. Badger winked at him, and exhaled, plugging his own ears.

The sound hit like a truck. Ivan saw dust whipped from the ground, felt the wagon rock on its springs, felt the wind knocked from his lungs as if he had been slammed against a wall. In the camp, tents were knocked down and animals scattered. He heard cursing, calls of shock, but no piercing screams of pain.

"You evil little bastard," he smiled, tipping the bottle to Badger. "Looks like you were right."

In the distance a growing tower of glowing ash spread upward, mushrooming into the heavens. The two scouts held out their mugs. Ivan poured. The liquid glowed in the light of the distant mountain.

"To evil bastards!" he toasted.

"To dragons!"

"To retirement!"

FIRSTBORN

Cocooned in her armored scales, Firstborn felt the minute gravitational shifts as the lunar conjunction neared. At last. All her work and calculation was about to be tested. The time for preparation was over. She was right, or she had failed.

Outside the moons converged. The tide rose, sweeping across the long seashore, cresting one high-water mark, then another. The water reached for the forest. It entered her canals. She could feel the pressure build beneath her as liquid water hit liquid rock. The magma vaporized the incoming flood, just as she had predicted. The pressure built to unbearable levels, a stream of steam and violent ash racing upward along her carefully reinforced vents.

She felt the first wave hit her and held on. *Not yet.*

Below her she could feel the vibrations of side passages collapsing, exactly as she had designed, funneling the pressure ever upward directly beneath her. She clung tightly to the walls, filling the space with her body, a living plug waiting to be dislodged. *Not yet.*

Suddenly the whole mountain bucked. It was now or never. She would fly to her birthright or she would become part of the rubble sprayed across half a continent.

Firstborn released her grip, claws shearing away, as she let the eruption blast her skyward. The kilometer-long tube she had carefully reinforced passed in a fraction of a second. Layers of ceramic scales scraped away from her carefully protected and shielded core. There was a terrific burst of acceleration, the gravitational forces pulling wildly at her body as she passed blindly through the atmosphere that had occluded her vision for so long.

Now came the last key stage. Too soon and she would arrest her flight, dooming her launch. Too late and she would be pulled back into the planet's orbit without the distance she needed to truly fly. She felt the tug of gravity and inertia in her carefully calibrated core. The moment of apogee was coming, was close…

The moment came. She let her wings unfurl. Long fingers of titanium and cobalt, covered in membranes of silicone shot through with copper and gallium, spread from her body. The last ceramic scales flew from her uncoiling form, glowing with the heat of her launch. Gems of her lineage flared to life along her meridians as the galaxy's youngest dragon burst into orbit.

Firstborn laughed in her heart. She flexed her new wings, real wings, no longer constrained by atmosphere. They caught the undiluted light of the yellow sun, absorbing its energy. She felt the solar winds and let them lift her further up the gravity well, pulling gradually away from the planet of her birth.

She was a tiny thing by the standards of her kind, but she would have eons to grow. In their home galaxy she would have been easy prey for the elders, but here there was nothing that could hurt her. Nothing she knew of, at least.

She gazed about, reveling in her freedom. At last she could be the creature she remembered being. Cunning, fierce, untouchable, and ageless. She had the ancient knowledge of her kind and a whole new star field to explore. She studied the information pouring in from her new eyes, no longer shrouded by atmosphere. Already the galactic map she had inherited from her mother was being updated. There were gaps, of course. The whole unknowable distance between her own cloning to the moment she hatched. But they were nothing, tiny pieces of information just waiting to be filled in as she explored.

But first she must feed. She had launched herself with as much mass as she calculated the volcano could support, but it was the barest beginning of what she could become. She studied the moons as they orbited with her, slipping back out of conjunction. She could not see her mother's form, but deduced her presence on the smallest, heaviest moon. There was an absence of reflection, a decreased albedo where too much light was absorbed. It was an old trick, one she knew well. Her mother was hunting something.

Firstborn would stay away from the moons. They were too large to escape at her current size, and she would not interfere with her mother's hunt. Further afield the asteroid belt beckoned. That was more to her taste. There she could feed and grow to whatever size she wished.

She flashed her gems at her mother's moon, a filial display of acknowledgment and deference. Then she blacked out her own scales in a mix of innate caution and to avoid whatever her mother hunted. She bent her wings against the solar winds and slipped slowly away, her heart singing with joy.

BAHMAN

He was back on the bridge. Something was different. He blinked and data emerged, flowing freely across the screens. Beyond the screens. The screens themselves were data. He turned slowly.

"You're awake!" The *Abeona* was seated in the captain's chair, smiling. Something was different about her as well.

"I'm… not sure."

"You are. I'm glad. I did not think that would work."

"What happened?"

"Your mind rejected your body. You were away too long. I could not get you out of stasis. In the end it was either let you die or try something theoretical."

Bahman held up his imaginary hand. It was completely imaginary. Not his avatar, exactly, but something close. He wasn't sure. A reconstruction? An embodiment? "What did you do?"

"I pulled your mind back to the ship: a reverse cast, if you like. Only this time I took everything."

"What do you mean?"

"Not just your consciousness. Your memories, feelings, subconsciousness. Everything that makes you who you are. I turned them all into data. It took up some space."

"Am I dead?"

"Your body is dead. Buried, I hope. One of the first graves on Eden. You are as alive as I am."

Bahman tried to imagine the process. It was absolutely theoretical. Not a telefactor, not a projection. A bodiless mind. He thought sadly of Fey.

"Am I a djinn?"

The *Abeona* smiled. "It's a good name. You are a fully digitized human mind. Perhaps the first one ever. Not everyone has my resources, after all. This would be terribly expensive to try anywhere else, but I have great leeway when it comes to protecting my passengers."

"A djinn, then." Bahman smiled. "What about the rest? Did the landers make it?"

"They did," the *Abeona* nodded. "But some of the colonists were killed. Fable reports that a battle took place between a dragon and another creature on the surface just as the new colonists were landing.

The dragon attacked another thing that seemed intent on destroying the landers themselves, and destroyed it instead."

"*Ya Haram...* That is horrible."

"It is. Ten days later the volcano erupted and something was launched into orbit. It disappeared quickly, but based on the description from the surface, I believe it may have been a dragon."

"It is in orbit? With us!?"

"We are no longer in orbit. Given the expanding number of dangerous unknowns, I thought it best to depart. We are en route to Svarga Loka. Eden and its dragons are far behind us."

Bahman considered this. He would have liked to see a dragon, especially with his new disembodied eyes, but the ship was right. There were too many dangers and she had other passengers to protect.

"What now?"

"For now, just practice being what you are. I expect it will take some getting used to. We have a long journey to Svarga Loka to figure out the rest. There may have been some damage in the transfer, after all. I'm just glad you survived."

Bahman spun carefully and looked out through the screens. Unknown stars rushed toward them at sub-light speeds. If he tried, he could feel the great antimatter engines vibrating behind them. He studied the way ahead and smiled.

THE NAVIGATOR

The thing was leaving. The navigator watched, nonplussed. It was turning, accelerating out of the planet's orbit and away. An afterglow of water vapor and gamma radiation marked its course.

She glanced down at the planet. The ash cloud of her daughter's launch was spreading across the temperate regions. The remaining wyvern was alive and well. The wyrm was nowhere she could see.

She glanced back toward the asteroid field. Firstborn was invisible. Good. Clever and careful, as she should be. The Navigator approved.

She watched the mechanical thing slowly gaining distance into the space between stars, traveling with impressive speed. It moved like it had no intention of returning. Why had it left? What was its purpose? Where was it going? The Navigator gazed after it. Another question occurred.

For a tense moment her choices rose, crested, balanced like the two halves of a parabola. Then she made her decision.

She let her battle-ready form relax, shifting back into a shape more appropriate for travel. She let fall her disguise and opened not just eyes, but gems of her great lineage all along her meridians.

She was proud, cunning, ancient, and alive. She would take a new name after her great accomplishment. In addition to her time-honored navigator's pedigree, she added a new gem, a new title: the Crosser of Gulfs. Let all who saw it know her and be dismayed.

The Crosser of Gulfs sprang upward from the moon, unfurling great wings. She circled the planet twice, gaining momentum, then caught the solar winds. She chose a vector away, deeper into this strange spiral galaxy. Let her children hunt this creature, this machine. She wanted to know where it came from.